Locked down
Bubbling up

Anthology of poetry and short stories

Mairead de Bhal, Mark Rice, Lesley Smith

2020

First published in November 2020

Published by Mairead de Bhal, Mark Rice, Lesley Smith
using www.kdp.amazon.com

Cover created using www.Wordart.com

Printed by www.amazon.com

www.Lockeddownbubblingup.wordpress.com

ISBN: 9798554481345

Walking
Zoom
Virus
Corona Virus
Corona Virus
Working from home
Working from home
Community
Replication
Travel restricted
TWO METERS
Teams
Garden
Zoom
Teams
DEATHS
Cases
Plasma
Economy
Baking
Gloves
Testing
Cocoon
Travel restricted
2020
Mask
Stay home
Lockdown
REOPENING
Election
Pods
Isolation
Vaccine
Jobs
Nursing Homes
Economy
Economy
TWO METERS
It will just disappear
It will just disappear
Gloves
Sanitiser
IF I GET IT I GET IT
STAYCATION
Ventilator
Ventilator
Beds
Ventilator
Jobs
Cocoon
Mask
Cases
Economy
2KM
2KM
FEAR
Mask
Clapping
IT IS WHAT IT IS
Toilet Roll
Covid 19
FRAMEWORK
Sunshine
Deaths
Garden
5KM
5KM
FEAR
Covid 19
Antibodies
Takeaway
STAYCATION
Community
Lockdown
Open the schools
Sunshine
HOME DELIVERY
Wash hands
Quarantine
Walking
Sanitiser

Acknowledgements

We thank our friends and families for encouraging us - Tiffy Allen for her inspiration, support and encouragement and Betty Lacey for her assistance with sourcing appropriate quotations.

We dedicate this book to the families that have been affected directly or indirectly by Covid-19, and to all those health care workers who have worked tirelessly at the forefront of this pandemic.

Table of Contents

Introduction

We are three writers who met in April 2020 through a zoom group at the start of the Covid-19 Pandemic in Ireland.

The March lockdown for us meant an effort to redeem something of ourselves during the restrictions.

We made a conscious effort to be creative, to write, to make sense of the world.

From a weekly meeting an idea evolved, something positive from something negative.

Locked down, away from our friends, family, jobs, routines, led us on a journey to local villages and beyond, to experience real and imagined.

We hope you enjoy reading our work, as much as we did writing it.

Stay well.

Mairead de Bhal, Mark Rice, Lesley Smith

"It's going to disappear. One day, it's like a miracle - it will disappear."

Donald Trump, 45th US President

Setting the scene

The year 2020 was a leap year. It started with conversations in Ireland on the sudden death of a much-loved radio presenter called Marian Finucane; and bush fires burning in Australia.

We complained about overcrowding in hospitals, the state exam marking process, lack of mental health services and the changes to pension age. The UK leaving the EU (Brexit) loomed while politicians were planning and discussing the formation of the new government. I was engrossed in a Psychology course and had holidays planned to go to France in March and Barbados in October. Life was good.

By mid-January, a faraway city in China called Wuhan and a new virus was causing concern but life in Ireland just carried on as usual.

In early February, Irish people living in China were advised to get ready to leave and thousands of cruise ship passengers were being quarantined. Those of us with cruises booked for our holidays looked on a bit alarmed and wondered if we might have to change our plans.

Discussions on viruses started and the benefits or otherwise of wearing masks began to emerge.

Storm Dennis washed an abandoned 'ghost ship' onto rocks off Co. Cork. The World Health Organisation stated, "China's coronavirus outbreak poses a very grave threat for the rest of the world and should be viewed as public enemy number one".

During March things were beginning to look concerning and our level of awareness increased. Hygiene and handwashing were a new focus.

Life changed dramatically on March 17th (St. Patrick's Day) when Leo Varadkar, our Taoiseach (Prime Minister) announced that significant steps would have to be taken to curb the spread of Covid-19. The first case in Ireland had been detected less than fourteen days before. Schools were to close and gatherings curtailed.

I remember watching the speech on television and inexplicably crying. I was not quite sure why but I think it was the realisation that this was going to affect my life and the lives of all my loved ones, in fact, all the world.

I was glad and proud to be Irish, glad to be living in Ireland and proud of our leaders, but fear was seeping into my mind. The WHO had declared that it was a Pandemic on March 12th but the message only really hit me that St. Patrick's Day 2020.

Lockdown followed and we learned a new language, virus, cocooning, self-isolating, R numbers and lots more became commonplace. We proudly stood and acted together.

School closures initially delighted pupils. People started working from home. The old and vulnerable were told to cocoon. I started ordering groceries online and having them delivered. I discovered Zoom and video features of What'sApp.

Misleading claims and information appeared on social media and we all hoped that something simple would be found to stop this in its tracks. I hoped for some miracle and that the virus would burn out in summer, alas that was not to be.

During the lockdown, the sun appeared. It was as if Mother Nature was saying, "Look all is not lost, the world is a beautiful place". We all walked miles in the sun and had takeaway coffee or tea at every opportunity with occasional meetings with friends or family sitting on the grass or walls, meters apart. We talked to loved ones from the end of the driveway or smiled and waved through closed windows. We all missed the hugs, kisses, pats on the back.

We craved meals out, trips to the pub, going to the weekly match. We baked, shared recipes, bemoaned the lack of flour, over-ate, over-drank and binge watched Netflix.

We developed a newfound admiration for nurses and doctors but also postmen, delivery people, carers. We looked for 'experts' and found some in the Public Health group (NPHET) we were Irish and we would do what was necessary to get through this.

We looked at other countries bemused by talk of herd immunity, civil liberties and protests. Black lives matter became a movement after the death of George Floyd in America. We were both entertained and appalled by statements made by the American President Donal Trump.

People worried about lives and livelihoods. The big question was how the two could be balanced. People lost income, jobs. Families struggled with 'working from home' versus 'childminding whilst at work'.

Relationships were fractured and lost or created anew over video calls. It was an opportunity to ring that long-forgotten friend or reconnect with lost family. Funerals took place without the normal support to the bereaved; the Irish wake was put on hold. Marriages were delayed or took please with reduced numbers of guests. The Leaving Certificate class of 2020 suffered in their assessment process and transition from second to third-level education.

The government created the plan to re-open up by stages and over time, life began to take on some semblance of normality in late summer. Wearing masks became the new normal in retail and indoor settings. Public houses were designated as 'acting as a restaurant' or 'wet'. Rules applied to everyday life! We took holidays consisting of a short break in another county in Ireland or a quick trip to a country on the Green List. Some risked more and broke the rules.

A big milestone was the reopening of schools in September, with a huge sigh of relief from parents and children alike.

Suffering covered not just those who contracted the virus but also those who could not access treatments or experienced cancellations and delays to critical health care needs. Many people lost jobs and educational opportunities. Many suffered societal bereavement as they could only watch life from the side-lines.

During September and early October, our virus cases began to rise again. The second wave had arrived. Ireland went back into Lockdown. Health experts warned that this virus may never go away and that we have to learn to live with it, with or without a vaccine. There was talk of vaccine developments that shone a light of hope. Understanding of the illness was improving all the time and treatments better understood.

Irish people experienced this year as a mixture of both the best and worst that we, as a people could be. We saw the Irish way challenged as never before. On occasions, we became judgemental, opinionated, suspicious and edgy. We became more caring, more aware and saw the best of people shine through the gloom. Uncertainty was the only certain thing. Different strata of society counted the cost and wondered who had fared worst.

We all shed tears, had fears, suffered losses in 2020 but we had good times too, we smiled, re-evaluated what was important. Some may change their lives or lifestyles because of lessons learned. Many things have been delayed or put on hold. I crave safety, travel but mostly the time when I can hug loved ones again.

We are resilient, we look forward in hope, humour and the knowledge that everything passes, and this will too.

Lesley Smith

"What seems to us as bitter trials are often blessings in disguise"

Oscar Wilde

Escaping to Lockdown

Fleeing like refugees,

not looking back,

praying that the Tsunami wave wouldn't catch us,

speeding to the safety of a refuge with a locked gate,

a view of the ocean to widen our frightened horizons.

Unpacking, the peace of the countryside calms our
rattled nerves.

The still trees smile at our hasty arrival and return
afterwards to their calm being.

The news at 9 pm tells it all, the whole country takes a
breath in,

it has arrived on our shores and we have to be vigilant.

We had read snippets about it on foreign shores

the photos of gown drenched overcrowded hospitals
reached us

we knew then, it was serious.

That first week we settled into a country rhythm,

working in the garden,

walking in the spring sun,

marvelling at the beauty around us.

Our purple fear seeped into the earth,

our oasis held us close, reassured us.

Visits to our elderly neighbours from the doorstep

were greeted with warmth and kindly concern,

all had been taken care of,

medications were delivered from the local pharmacy

a weekly box of food from the local village shop

meant life continued on

At night the sea roars, despite the strength,

its rhythm cooling and strong,

lulling us to sleep, protecting us,

Nothing makes sense anymore.

Life has stopped in the last few months, as we know it.

Our brothers and sisters of all colours now wear surgical masks,

children are warned not to come too close.

stay in your own bubble we are warned.

More restrictions follow.

The birds on the feeder flying in all directions feast happily,

Swooping in, their excited song fills the air.

Their impatient feeding brings a joy, a playfulness

to this now Halloween containment.

Confined to quarters, I busy myself in activities

that I always wanted to do,

My sister knits happily listening to easy Saturday radio.

Autumnal orange vegetables roast in the oven.

It's the luck of the draw.

Born in the right place,

with the opportunity to run,

to get ahead,

to move sideways,

dodge the bullets,

Born where doors open,

we have choices,

we exercise some power over our lives,

The choice to lockdown, a necessary precaution

against a danger, to protect us.

We are not locked out,

not out in the cold, or frozen,

or drowning in the Mediterranean seas,

Not abused and humiliated

or beaten to a pulp because of our colour; our sex; our religion.

I open the window to let the sea air into the room,

It freshens the space, and its coldness sends a shiver up my spine.

My fragile heart trembles and waits.

Mairead de Bhal

From Plymouth Rock to Rhode Island Red

That was it.

Michael had saved and saved every penny. He had counted it, over and over, 6 euros return and 20 euros for the book. Mam had said he could go in on his own, as long as he got the early bus, and came back at 4 o'clock.

He couldn't sleep the night before. His mother prepared his breakfast and looked out the window for John, his cousin, who worked in the city.

He arrived at exactly 8.45am and rang the doorbell. Michael flew out to him, kissing his mam on the cheek and promising to see her at 4 o'clock. His first trip on his own.

Very few of his friends ever took the bus; they went into town in their family cars. It never bothered him. They had no place to park a car anyways Mam always said. It had come up in a class discussion about family cars, he remembered when it was his turn, he couldn't think of what to say. Maistear Byrnes had noticed his hesitancy and quickly passed him by. Michael remembered the sense of relief.

The older youth pushed him up the stairs of the bus. They nabbed the front seat, since the bus turned around just beyond the village, and they were the first on board for the return journey. Michael sat back and looked in amazement. The sweep of soft hills and the sea beyond. The view so different from up here. This was his place, his home, his world.

John knew the next passenger who sat across from them and they chatted easily about the Sunday game. Michael stared out at the quiet cows looking gently as the bus sailed up and down the windy roads, along the sea road.

The next village gave more passengers up to the bus- old ladies with shopping bags and passes, and laughing teenage girls with makeup and handbags.

The lively chatter of everyone rang in Michael's ears, and his eyes marvelled at the busyness of the city streets. He saw a nun walking across the road, making her way to a large church; some girls in miniskirts, one of them winked at him, he looked around to see if John saw her, but he hadn't, he wouldn't want John to see him blush. Just as he was recovering, John gave him a dig in the ribs. They had arrived at the station, the bus swung slowly around into the bay, like a piglet into a pen.

The minute his feet hit the pavement, he was dazed, with the crowd. His cousin broke the spell, grabbing his elbow and steering him on. They found a space, brushing past a black couple.

The man's massive muscles reminded Michael of a wrestler, from the Saturday night wrestling. He had a shiny tee shirt and a large golden chain, and the brightest of white teeth. He was laughing with a large lady dressed in a swath of robes. His huge tummy went up and down, when he laughed, and his face glistened shiny like a sliotar on a wet morning. The woman was fierce-looking, a turban cloth on her head, a red dress and enormous beaded earrings. When she grinned up at the man, her earrings made a tiny chiming sound.

Distracted, he dropped his bus ticket and, bending down to lift it up, he stared into a pair of serious brown oval eyes. She was sitting on a weekend case, with her hands on her round pigtailed head reading. Calm and deep, she looked back at him. He lifted the ticket and found himself for a second caught in her gaze.

Her expression softened and she smiled. John pulled him up quickly. Michael looked back; she was peering after him through her father's legs. He wanted to go back and ask her name but John was pushing him onwards.

They were out on the street, and he pointed in the direction of the river. The bookshop is up there, he said, as he took off for work in the opposite direction. Michael shook himself, realising that he was on his own, in the city. The grey stone with a glint of silver like the sea in the early morning bounced back at him, he squinted and held his head high to see if he could catch any landmarks. He saw the name of a street he recognised from the instructions his cousin had given him earlier. Turning to the left, he then had to take a sharp right, coming out at a T junction, he spotted the bookshop with the funny sign Mc Kenzies, the oldest bookshop in the county, founded in 1880's and going strong ever since.

When he pushed the green door, a brass bell tinkled behind him. The quietness shocked him and the smell, like a wall of lavender in early summer. He stopped for a moment to breathe, this was the moment he had planned, he had longed for, that had kept him awake in the dark winter evenings, long after his mother had fallen asleep, and he could hear her snoring across the corridor.

The rows of bookshelves reaching to the ceiling, leading to cool soft hushed corners, with small reading stools. The mahogany polished wooden counter stretched the length of the shop and stopped at a large window where the River Drule could be seen shining and lazily twisting to the sea. The warm orange earthed tiled floor, shone with love, lent a reverence to your walking. A deliberate short cough startled him out of his reverie.

A white-shirted young man leaned over the counter. He wore a blue-spotted dicky bow, and his blonde hair was in a ponytail like a costume one of the clowns wore at the summer circus that bundled into town on the August bank holiday weekend. He cleared his throat again. "Can I help you?"

Michael hesitated trying to prevent himself from laughing out loud. He steadied himself and remembered why he was there. He breathed and in the smallest of voices, even though he tried to speak louder he said. "Yes." There was a silence, the young pony-tailed counter assistant, kept looking at him and nodding encouraged by his answer.

"I've ordered The Plymouth Rock to Rhode Island Red Adventure, and I'm here to collect," Michael said as quickly as he could, his heart pounding.

The hard-backed tome landed on the table with a slight thump. Yellow covered, it was one foot by one foot and reprinted 23 times since it was first published one hundred years ago. Still, as relevant as ever, the reviews read.

Michael opened it silently, and at once recognised the drawings and photographs from the internet. He felt himself suddenly becalmed.

He closed the book and put his palm on the cover for a few seconds. He might have stayed like that for a while except that the fidgety assistant asked whether he wanted it gift wrapped, "Yes," he replied. "In the best paper you have," he added confidently.

He handed over his money, and received the precious goods, turned and walked slowly out to the sunny morning. As the door closed with a gentle tinkle, Michael knew he would come back here, and frequent the coffee shop at the back.

His step was lighter, yet surer, as he surveyed the street names and navigated his way back to the station.

Suddenly profoundly tired, feeling the book under his arm and holding on tight, he found a seat. He must have nodded off when he felt a brush against his knee. "Is this your bus?" she said.

He looked up, there she was, the girl with the serious eyes. He glanced at the board, five minutes to go, he nodded. The door of the bus remained closed as the driver prepared for his journey out the peninsula.

"I'm getting the same one," she said. She stood up, and so did he. She was the same height, her body tall and thin. She had gold earrings that framed her sincere face, and those braided pigtails. She was wearing blue tracksuit top, white leggings with runners. Under the top, he could just see a light blue t-shirt, with a pink border. She leaned her head on her side, and looked at him and then at the book.

"What's that?"

"A book," he replied.

"What sort of book?"

"It's about rearing and minding hens," he replied. She stared.

He saw her parents making their way to the starting queue, "I'm moving out here," she said. "It's going to be our new home. Starting in St Raphael's in September."

"I go there," he replied.

"Oh," she said. She was silent for a minute. "I want to be a scientist, and find a cure for cancer," she said.

"Where are you from," he asked.

"I'm from Portlaoise, but I was born in Nigeria."
Her parents called her then, and she left, glancing back,

"Good luck with your hens. I'm Skye, what's your name?"

"Michael." He said.

He saw her at the end of the bus wedged in the back seat between her parents. He waved at her, and she smiled. Michael wondered whether she might like a chicken when he had his business up and running.

Dad had loved hens, and after he left, Mam had chopped the chicken run up for firewood. He'd often come home, and she would be slapping the bread on the counter when she was baking, she'd toss and throw the bread on the wooden table like a living thing, and beat it like a bodhran He was afraid of the expression edged sharply on her face, not that she would do something to him, but that maybe she might do something to herself, it was a feeling he had. He had heard rumours that his father had left for England, with money troubles.

People talked sideways in the village, but no one really ever looked in his eye and told him what had happened. Nobody ever explained what happened that night he disappeared. His mother was in denial and shock. A terrible shame fell upon their home. He had gone numb, for years after, when he thought of his father. He knew he had to take care of his mother. He always tried his best in school he thought that would cheer her up, and he helped her with the sticks for the fireplace, and washed his dishes.

He'd go straight to his room those days when she was banging the dough. And come out on tippy-toes, and talk to her about his day, she would sit wearily smiling up at him from the chair beside the range.

Michael began remembering his father telling him how to mind hens in the dark winter evenings, when he was alone. His father used to explain gently how to feed them and water them and most importantly protect them from the fox. He distinctly heard his father's voice explain the two varieties, Plymouth Rock and Rhode Island Red. His father took his hand and taught him how to lift the soft hens, and not to upset them. "Gently, Gently, son," he'd whispered. Michael's heart would ache for the touch. He missed his father, but he couldn't talk to his mother about it.

The idea of hens seemed to take hold of him over the last few months. He woke up with their names on his lips. He'd say the names over and over Plymouth Rock, Rhode Island Red, Plymouth Rock, Rhode Island Red. When he repeated them over, he thought of his father, he tried to picture his face and he wondered where he was now, was he alive or dead, did he have another family, did he rear hens?

His father had talked of his own father having this great book, but he was never able to afford one. Today, Michael had one; he felt it against his chest.

Heavy and real. He wondered would his father be proud of him, the special book bought with his own money.

His mother would be waiting for him, she might be angry, maybe frown, but he really hoped she would give in. His eyes grew weary with the sway of the bus, sashaying through the hot country roads, rocking him like his mother did when he was a baby. He found his eyes closing, and he dreamt of eggs, Rhode Island Reds, and the sound of a cock a doodle doo.

Mairead de Bhal

*"If you can't explain it simply, you
don't know it well enough"*

Albert Einstein

True or false

An IF met a MAYBE and said I like your BUT,

the IF became certain it was not as simple as it looked.

It might have been a falsehood or maybe just a spin,

the info it was based on came from a source within.

The evidence was invalid, DATA incomplete,

the protocol applied came from out of state.

Trying to extrapolate might perpetrate a crime,

the survey was paid for, the study was not blind,

the bias not considered, the finding far from sound,

the BUT was getting bigger, still IF hung around.

The MODEL was questioned, the science in dispute,

replication a feature finding a square root.

OUTCOME turned to face the facts,

not always based on truth.

FACT had many features with errors at it's root.

GRAPH came in to clarify so that we could see,

maps, bars and pie charts did their best indeed.

CERTAINTY left the room, EVIDENCE did a dance

sometimes you could see her even at a glance.

In the end the MAYBE met up with the BUT,

IF realised that trends can at times be bucked.

INFERENCE was testing at random in their range

he skewed the mean to represent something very strange

ESTIMATE was faulty, PROBABILITY insane.

PERCENTAGE then decided to analyse their pain.

MAYBE met EQUATIONS waiting by the door.

IF and BUT retracted leaving DATA on the floor.

Lesley Smith

Alone

Joe stepped out of the downpour and into the shop doorway. Carefully he removed his gloves storing them in his coat pocket. He shook vigorously displacing a gallon of water from his coat. Blowing the chill off his hands, he grabbed a metal basket and headed up the first aisle. He couldn't help noticing the increasingly empty shelves.

"Bread" he muttered and threw a sliced loaf into the basket. It was promptly joined by a box of eggs and three litres of milk. He took only a small bag of potatoes and a small jar of coffee, as he wouldn't squeeze anything bigger into the rucksack. Along the second aisle, he trod and into his basket went a bag of carrots, a pot of strawberry jam and a jar of organic honey.

He'd made to the third aisle before he met another human. Mary sat hunkered on the floor adding price stickers to a box of bottled shampoo.

"Morning Mary, it's monsoon season again," Joe, said smiling at the young woman.

"That it is Joe" she replied, "and aren't we the lucky ones to be enjoying it?"

"We surely are," he answered grabbing a tin of mushy peas off the nearby shelf.

"Why is there someone missing out on this wonderful morning?" he asked.

"Haven't you heard?" said Mary with a surprised look. "Batty, from across the road died suddenly at home yesterday and Mrs Lynch passed away in Wexford General on Monday evening. Her removal is this morning from Wallaces."

"Lord, I knew of Mrs Lynch but Batty is a shock to me. She hadn't the virus had she?" Joe asked.

"No Joe, as far as I know, she hadn't but she had it hard after Richard died from it last year. From that moment onwards, it was as if life held nothing for her. I never saw her smile again. Sure only last Sunday she was in here getting her bits and pieces, a lovely woman, God rest her soul," answered Mary.

"Indeed," said Joe and he went to move on past her.

"Afore you go Joe," she said in a whisper, "If you look on the shelf behind the ATM you'll find two bottles of Jameson. I saved them for you when the delivery came in last week."

"Don't forget now," she warned with a smile "God knows when another load will come in" and he gave her the thumbs up.

He strode on into the next aisle and noted the freezer section had been switched off for good now. He grabbed the last tube of toothpaste, hummed, and hawed over the newspaper and magazines section eventually buying a colouring book.

Mary had been as good as her word and Joe collected the bottles. He made his way to the checkout picking up a bag of porridge on the way.

"Morning Joe, fierce day isn't?" Padraig said as he scanned Joe's basket.

"Surely is Padraig, I heard about Batty just now. That's a bit of a shocker eh?"

"Forty-nine euro if you please Joe. Aye, we were not expecting that to happen and that's for sure."

"No point in offering you a fifty?" Joe asked.

"No, you can keep your fifty Joe. No one wants notes anymore. You know that."

"Just flash that card now like a good man" replied Padraig.

"I'll do it but I'm not sure there's much in there!" replied Joe. He slid the card over the reader and they both held their breath and waited. After some hesitation, the paper role began to spew forth so they both knew there was enough in the bank, at least for Joe today.

"Keep well" were Padraig's last words.

"You too and give my best to your better half," said Joe as he carefully packed away his purchases.

Minutes later Joe walked out of the shop, his bulging rucksack strapped to his back. The heavy rain showed no sign of letting up. It had taken a good hour and a half to walk there and now it would be the same going home but he didn't mind, as it was a form of therapy, exercising his mind while his body got a workout. Sometimes he thought up some great ideas during the walk and sometimes the walk served only to remind him that he needed a new pair of wellington boots.

The water came through a hole in the sole of his right boot. He'd known of the problem setting off and had stuffed a J-cloth in the boot to soak up the water but right now, his sock was also a cold wet mess. The elastic had gone from it too and it had slipped down his shin to lie with the J-cloth in the toe of his boot. Boots were just two more things that you couldn't get any more for love nor money.

He braced himself for the walk home and set off past the hardware store walking across its empty petrol forecourt. It had closed when they ran out of petrol, coal and near about anything you'd need to complete a DIY job. That was two years ago.

On he walked now passing the Post Office, which shut shortly after Mary O'Brien, the postmistress, died and wasn't replaced. Next to it was the hairdresser who never re-opened after the fifth wave of infection. Next again was Bridges pub which had been due to open in phase four, three years ago but never did. Crossing the road he left the small shopping centre behind its car park well on the way to becoming a lake.

Joe walked on down the hill and past the busiest man in the village, the undertaker. Though he'd buried thousands, Tom Wallace still evaded death himself.

Joe glanced between the entrance pillars and peered up the driveway through the driving rain that bounced off the pebbles. There was Tom now with his team of helpers at the rear of the hearse loading a coffin. Dressed in full PPE gear the team Joe thought they moved like men-walking-on-the-moon, taking slow and deliberate steps in a choreographed dance.

One stood back from the rest and used a camera to record the event. Joe presumed Mrs Lynch's family were watching it all from home. Next stop would be the graveyard and no one would be there at the graveside save Tom and his team. Not even a priest to attend and deliver a final blessing. They had to prioritise their time and the needs of the living won out over the dead.

"I wonder where he gets his petrol from." asked Joe of himself as he turned away and resumed his journey.

Joe had a car and it sat in his driveway this past ten years. He ran the engine once a month to keep life in the battery.

He'd last filled up the tank when? Was it last year or the year before? Anyway, he had kept it ready for an emergency, for if he got ill and had to visit the hospital.

Last Christmas some bastards had visited one night and broken the lock on the petrol cap. They drained his fuel tank so now he had just the jerry cans hidden in the shed with the petrol he'd kept for the tractor. He'd put a bit in the car so he could continue to turn the engine over but he was no longer sure he could reach the hospital with what he had left.

On down the hill, he walked at eleven am on a working day in September 2023 and not a soul to see. Mind you, don't ask him which day it was, as he couldn't tell you. Time for Joe had become a vaguely familiar matter. In the context of his life, days had ceased to matter so he no longer noted their passing.

He glanced into the windows of the houses he now passed and noticed the red sticker in more than half of them. Each time he visited the village there were more red stickers. He had a similar one in his window now.

Joe had now reached the bottom of the hill and stood at the centre of the village. The road widened out and a large open paved area lay to his right. In summer this place used to rock with the sound of music and song. He could recall the tinkle of glasses carried out by waitresses to the tables set outdoors under the dappled moonlight. The smell of freshly cooked food used to fill his nostrils. Above all, there came the voices of villagers, many of whom were no longer with us.

"Will we ever see the village alive again?" he wondered.

He had to turn out and away from the village now. The only positive he could take from the relentless rain was that it came straight down and not into his unprotected face. The road now began to rise and he was nearing the Farmers Co-Op which lay in total darkness. It had kept going as long as it could but sure, with no replenishment of stock it had to close.

Joe now reached the last three houses on the edge of the village which all lay empty. Estate agent signs stood tall nailed to tall poles tied to gateposts.

One had been for sale before the pandemic hit and had even gone sale agreed but then the purchaser died and back onto the market it went again. Joe had thought about selling their place but the initial fleeing from cities by Dublin residents had proved to be a short-lived fad.

Dublin still had supplies of food and petrol, Dublin still had goods for sale in its shops, Dublin still had money. It was the same old story for the rural dwellers across the island, being forgotten and treated as second class citizens by urbanite governments.

Now his walk transitioned from urban living to rural living. He went from well-lit roads with pavements to roads with no pavements and no lights. He switched on his headlamp and even at this early hour his tiny bulb fought to illuminate the road ahead. Misty waves of rain that continued to fall. His high-viz jacket made him extremely visible to any traffic but he hadn't been passed by any on the outward leg and wasn't expecting any different now.

He'd made it past Connolly's field and was approaching Roches cabin when a tractor with a trailer pulled up alongside him and the cabin door swung invitingly open.

"Joe, Joe step up here you silly bugger," said a voice. It was Nicky Furlong his neighbour.

"Feck sake man if you'd told me you were off to the village I'd have driven you down," said Nicky storing Joe's rucksack away behind the passenger seat. "It's raining cats and dogs out there. Get your arse up here!"

Joe climbed up the steps leaning heavily against the giant tractor tyre as he went. He ignored Nicky's verbal onslaught and proceeded to lower his hood and unzip his coat. Nicky put the tractor in gear and away they went warm and dry inside the cabin.

"How's you been Joe?" said Nicky as he peered ahead through the driving rain and swishing wipers. "Geraldine was asking about you only this morning and I said I'd seen your light on yesterday so I reckoned you were still about."

"Aye, I'm fine Nicky, missing Noleen of course. I'm still figuring out how to use the washing machine and I haven't had an oven-cooked meal in eighteen months!"

"You're a sentimental bastard Joe ain't that the truth of it?" laughed Nicky.

"Of course I miss her Nicky. It's just I find it hard expressing myself" replied Joe, now a tad embarrassed.

"You fine?" he asked of Nicky.

"We're all good" Nicky replied, "but I was worried about you especially when you both got it."

"I had a few rough days and that's for sure but I came through it. Now I'm still short of breath, especially at night but the doc got me a special facemask yoke a few months back. It blows air into my nose all night which helps with the breathing but it can be fierce uncomfortable. I often disconnect from it if I move about in the bed in me sleep. Other than that, I'm fine Nicky. Missing Noleen goes without saying after twenty years together but I'm also missing Lady of course."

"Ah yes, Lady she was a fine dog. She's gone sure it must be six months now?" said Nicky. "No news from the guards?"

"Still nowt Nicky and I'm not optimistic. I thought I'd be hearing something by now. She truly was a one-in-a-million dog. She's out there somewhere with those bastards now" said Joe.

"Apparently there was a gang operating in the Wexford area and they drove around in a van kidnapping dogs to sell in England. And for vast sums of money," said Nicky. "Anyway that's what's been said," he added.

"Here you are then Joe," said Nicky pulling up outside a nineteen fifty's style bungalow. Further up the driveway sat an ageing silver Ford Escort and behind the house stood a tall corrugated barn. It housed Joe's winter fodder and his tractor.

Joe stepped down carefully from the tractor and Nicky passed him down his rucksack.

"Now don't be a stubborn bastard and promise me next time you'll give me a call if you need some shopping," shouted Nicky before driving off. Joe gave him a wave and promptly stepped away from the tractor and trailer, which sent a wave of water his direction.

Joe walked up the driveway and put his key in the front door. He stepped inside his hallway and switched on the light whilst shedding his saturated coat and waterlogged wellingtons. He took his rucksack into the kitchen, threw on the light and unpacked his purchases on the wooden table.

He turned the kettle on and poured some instant coffee into a cup and while the water came to the boil, he started up his laptop and visited his Gmail account.

"No post today baby Janc" he muttered "Shame on them."

He glanced over to the empty dog bed in the corner and the torn blanket that Lady used to love to chew on.

He packed the last of the food away and had drunk most of his coffee when he spotted the colouring book still lying on the table. He reached into a kitchen cupboard and poured some cornflakes into a bowl. He added some cold milk and a sprinkling of sugar to the bowl. Now he took out a breakfast tray he'd given to Noleen one Christmas. He placed the bowl, spoon and drawing book on it and walked back into the hall.

There he rapped on the cupboard door and shouted: "stand back, stand back!"

He opened the door and pushed the tray into the small room lit by a single light bulb. There in the far corner, a young boy of fifteen or so huddled beneath a blanket and stared back at him.

"Stay back now until that door is closed" he warned grufly.

"Please mister" he shouted, "let me go!"

"Not till I get Lady back from your pals" Joe answered for the hundredth time his face emotionless and made of stone. He stepped back closing the cupboard door once more, twisting the key in the lock.

"How was he coping in these exceptional days?" he asked himself as he changed clothes upstairs in his bedroom. "I'm really doing fine."

Mark Rice

Leaving a legacy

"I've made 39 holes in this marshy field," he said excitedly.

"The apple trees are coming from Wexford this afternoon."

He would make apple juice, cider, and bake tarts.

The grandchildren would shelter under the branches from the summer sun.

"The holes are too big though,

The wrong bucket is on the digger.

Sure it's no problem to back -fill them by hand.

It's just extra work."

He sighed.

"But it's good work, isn't it?

What else would you be doing?"

He smiled and pushed his cap back on his head,

a trickle of sweat dripping down the lines of his cheeks.

He limped back to his work.

Mairead de Bhal

"Asking the question 'are we doing enough' regularly and repeatedly is critical."

Dr Maria Van Kerkhove, World Health Organisation

March 12th 2020

Pandemic announced

One cute Cute Hoor

It was a miserable dark wet evening in February when Neil turned the key in the lock and shut his shop on Kilgordan Main Street.

"Do you need a lift?" he heard from over his shoulder and turned to find Mary locking up her hairdressing business next door.

He smiled warmly back at her and said "No, you're fine Mary, Bride is picking me up on the way past in five minutes. I'll just stand under the bus shelter over there until she gets here."

"How was it today for you?" he asked.

She pulled her coat hood up over her blonde hair and tightened the strings in a knot under her chin, before walking over to answer him. "Ah, sure I was busy enough but next week is shaping up to be manic. With Saint Valentine's Day falling on a Friday I'll have to get Deidre in for a few days to help me."

How about you? How is the book business?" she asked.

"Ah, a bit quiet if I'm honest." It was only his third week of trading and he was still feeling his way.

"Don't you worry Neil. There's been a bookshop in this town for decades and Matty had the place buzzing last Christmas. Once the regulars get to know you and the fact that the shop's open again, I'm sure the till will be humming," she said smiling before turning to head for her car.

He waved as she went and then stood outside the shop for a few minutes, examining his front windows with a critical eye. Then he moved further back and took in the sea blue masonry paint he'd applied to the exterior brickwork before focusing in on the wooden embossed black lettering of "Blue Books, trading since 1912." Aye, it looked every bit the real thing.

Sure, his window display could do with sprucing up but that's to be expected. He'd planned to catch the Valentine's Day mood tomorrow with a few chick-lit novels displayed casually lying across a velvet pink cushion covered by a scattering of tiny pink hearts. A few balloons lay in the back room for inflating and he'd detonate a streamer over the lot and the cascading colourful twirled paper would dangle off anything they landed on. Maybe he'll run an offer of three romance novels for ten euro for the coming week.

The scrutiny over, he moved to stand under the bus shelter and searched the oncoming headlamps for Bride's car. He thought back to the moment he'd purchased the business and Matty was one cute hoor alright. He'd driven a hard bargain once he knew Neil was hooked. He'd known that Neil was a life long civil servant with an itch to scratch, an urge to take a chance at running his own business, of being his own boss.

"Neil, my price for the business was for buying the freehold and the shop name now, a name with an unrivalled history of book selling in Ireland."

"Jesus, at that price you got a bargain and that's a fact but" and he shook his head sadly, "the stock is extra my friend!"

"That's another twenty-five big ones but for that" and he looked Neil squarely in the eye "you are getting thousands of quality books in a stock that goes back a century or more."

"Sure people come for miles just to see them and book collectors are at my door daily pressing me to sell them." "Aye you're getting a bargain there Neil.""I may change me mind now, just thinking about it"

He paused and pondered for a moment. Neil tensed up, fearing the deal was off, but then Matty smiled.

"No, I gave you my word and that my bond"

He shook Neil's hand vigorously. Aye one cute hoor was Matty.

Anyway, Matty had enjoyed a good last Christmas in the shop with the doorbell ringing loudly and frequently. He said he'd give Neil training on the job, free gratis and for nothing. What he meant was Neil became Matty's shop assistant and gofer for the month. At least Neil got an opportunity to meet the shops regular customers but Matty worked him long and hard, opening the shop seven days a week right up to New

Years-eve when, outside on the pavement he locked up and handed the keys to Neil. Neil hadn't seen sight nor sound of Matty since.

Bride honked the horn and Neil looked up and saw her car just feet away. He ran through the puddles and slipped into it.

"Hi ya love, how was business today?" she asked as he settled in his seat.

"Fine" was all he said and she didn't drill deeper as the six o'clock news had started on the radio and they both listened intently to it during the fifteen minute drive home.

He was glad she dug no deeper as he didn't want to worry her about the shop. He was actually burning through their savings at an astonishing rate. He'd saved where he could but the real costs like council tax, water rates, insurance and utilities charges and of course Matty's price were unavoidably hitting the bank.

Only today, he had to pay fifty euro to an author who popped in. It was beginning to appear to Neil that a lot of the books he'd bought as stock could turn out to be books that Matty didn't actually own. Apparently, in the book business, its common practice that stock is supplied on a sale or return basis. It means that if he sold a copy of the book for twelve euro then the supplier/ writer gets eight euro and he is left with only four euro. He was a worried man.

The next day Bride dropped him off at 9:00 am and he spent the first hour on his first front window display, a daily chore, endeavouring to capture passing interest. The rest of the week passed quietly with the highlight being the delivery of the latest Marian Keyes novel, "Grown Ups", which had six customers waiting outside his door when he arrived on Thursday morning. He could do with a few more books like that.

The following day, on Friday evening, he hosted his first book launch and stayed open an extra two hours to facilitate a local author, David Doyle, to launch his book "Alone Again." It was a fictional story of love, betrayal, more love, a heap full of lust, a smidgen of unrequited love and then betrayal, again. It wasn't Neil's cup of tea but it was rumoured all over town that the book was more a work of fact than fiction. Indeed, a few of the locals bought copies on the belief that they were recognisable within the characters that populated the work. The author neither confirmed nor denied the stories, which itself did no harm to the book sales. Whatever the buyer's reason for buying, he sold more than one hundred copies of the book that night and for the first time, on the way home he allowed himself to believe that "Blue Books" could actually make money.

He did a steady trade the next week and as the month drew to a close, things were looking up for the little shop. It was the last Saturday in February when he hopped into Bride's car at 6:00 pm and they both heard of the first case of Covid-19 in the country. Some school kid had taken a ski holiday in Northern Italy and come home infected. It had been just one story in the news still dominated by the failure of political parties to form a Government and frankly, they switched off the radio and talked about food for dinner that night.

The following Monday on their drive to work, they heard that Google were going to let thousands of their staff in Ireland work from home as one staff member had developed flu-like symptoms.

"Jesus, that's over-cooking it" said Neil, "sure there's only been one proven Covid infection in the entire country. Google must have more money than sense. People will never work as hard at home as in the office. The business will go to pot. Mark my words they'll be dragging them all back to Dublin city in a fortnight's time!"

Bride, if she had disagreed held her tongue and watched as he waved her away and blew a kiss. She smiled as she drove on "You're an old romantic you."

Life continued as normal in Kilgordan that week. Neil took in a large delivery of books. A change to the intermediate-certificate reading list for English led to him selling out of William Shakespeare's "Julius Caesar" however, in the wider world, by the end of the week the number of infections in the country was now eighteen and one of those was a health worker.

"You must be careful Bride" said Neil on hearing the news that Sunday night "There may be something to this virus story."

"I am Neil and I promise I'll be careful in future too," she answered petulantly.

"Only this week Doctor Brown told me he has ordered some PPE equipment for the practice. I'm to be given a face visor as I'm on reception and I'm being put in charge of the liquid sanitiser and the paper towels. Extra responsibility equals extra money eh?"

"I don't believe that for a second" said Neil "But don't turn it down if he offers."

"You better get yourself sorted too" said Bride "and don't forget to keep your distance from customers and wash your hands." Neil nodded but he didn't actually change his ways. Covid-19 to him was an invisible threat, something like a bad dose of the flu that was occurring in Dublin almost two hundred miles away.

It took the Government cancelling of St. Patricks Day in early March that brought it home to him. He'd decorated the shop window with shamrocks and had placed religious books about the good saint in prime position in the shop. He'd high hopes for book sales on the day. The annual local parade was usually well attended by a couple of thousand out-of-towners and the parade went past his door. He'd even purchased a tall tricoloured hat to wear himself but with only ten days to go the Government pulled the plug countrywide.

Two days later the Government ordered universities, schools, and child care centres to close for seventeen days. Ireland had suffered the first death on the island. Within minutes of the Taoiseach's announcement, across the country, people were clearing the supermarket shelves of food, drink and toilet rolls. Neil stood gazing out his shop window at the supermarket across the road where you'd swear they were giving the food and drink away. People were exiting with trolleys overflowing only to jump in cars that waited double parked outside. He marvelled at the almost feverish activity whilst feeling depressed that his store currently lay silent and empty. If only he'd decided to sell groceries and not books. Aye one cute hoor was Matty Doyle.

Neil reached into his jacket and glanced at his latest business bank statement. It showed his current account balance was now less than €10,000. This was what was left of his retirement lump sum. He could talk up the sales to Bride and anyone who would listen but the bank account never lied. He turned out the lights and set the alarm that night worried for the first time about his new business.

Three days later the Government ordered pubs and hotel bars to close temporarily, for a fortnight but before the month of March was over the message was work from home, the closure of schools and child care facilities was extended to mid-April and the state had 2,475 confirmed cases of Covid-19 reported up until midnight on Sunday, 28 March.

"Love, shouldn't you stay at home today?" Bride tactfully asked Neil one morning while they dressed in their bedroom.

"Why?" he asked whilst focusing on lacing up his shoes.

"The Government says only people providing essential services should go to work" she replied "and as I'm working the medical practice I have to go but you don't."

"Well, it's essential for us that I go to the shop and sell a few books" he replied. "I mean how can we survive on just your salary?"

"Why don't you ring Social Welfare and see if you qualify for the Government Covid-19 emergency income payment?" she said. So he did when he got into the shop that morning but they said it only applied to employees laid off. Apparently three hundred thousand had already applied successfully but he wasn't going to be one of them.

He took his usual post on a high stool perched behind his window display and sipped his coffee whilst gazing out on the cobbled street before him. He exchanged cheery waves with several passers-by and then the street went quiet and for a full minute no pedestrian or vehicle passed. Shortly after ten, Mister Postman gave him a friendly nod but just kept walking. Mary also swept past managing a hurried half wave and pointing at her watch before disappearing from eyesight. Now the street became silent once more. He vowed to bring a small radio in tomorrow, as the silence was depressing.

He washed his cup in the small kitchen out the back and heard the doorbell tinkle over the front door.

He dropped the tea towel and saw a scruffy looking man walking briskly towards his cash desk.

"Can I help you?" Neil asked as he arrived a touch breathless at the desk, ahead of the shopper.

"No mister. I was planning to have a look around and see what you got" the man said his eyes darting around the room, taking in the expanse of books and shelves.

"Sure go ahead" Neil replied, relaxing a little. "Don't hesitate to call me if you need any assistance."

The man acknowledged the offer and proceeded to wander about the shop for the next hour and more. Sometimes he'd stop and open a book and read from it for ten minutes or more before putting it back. Two hours on, he showed no sign of leaving and had settled on a small stool, in the far corner of the shop, coincidentally next to the rooms only source of warmth, a three bar gas heater. As time passed, they'd exchange glances but not words. Neil was beginning to wonder what he could do now that he had a lodger on the premises.

Suddenly the doorbell rang and a real customer walked in with her daughter, a small girl in school uniform, he'd guess about thirteen. "Have you a copy of "Tales of Witchcraft" by William Wallace?" the youngster asked and smiled warmly at him. Her mother stood proudly behind her, hands resting on the child's shoulders.

"I believe I do," answered Neil with a matching smile and together the three walked down the shop to a stand just opposite the scruffy lodger. Neil gazed along the rows of paperback books in the Children's Section. He searched by T and then by W but there was no sign of the book. He knew he had it but where had it gone?

"Could you excuse me for a minute while I check my store out the back? I just know I have a copy so please bear with me," Neil asked and off he went. Out of sight to the others, Neil virtually tore the shelves apart as he searched vainly for the book. By the time he'd given up the search and returned to the shop proper the pair had left. He had to admit he'd been more than a minute but still........

"Ya just missed them" said the man from over his shoulder. Neil now noticed that the man was standing with his old coat flung open and was toasting himself and his undergarments in front of the flickering flames from the gas heater.

"I can guess why they've left" Niall said loudly. "I mean, how long have you been standing like that?" "Cover yourself up man for Gods sake!" he ordered.

And that's when he smelt it! His nose now picked up for the first time the very strong pungent smell of male un-washed body odour. An odour that had matured over several days was now being unleashed in his shop. No wonder the others had left in a hurry!

"You—out now!" Neil shouted to the man.

He hurriedly wrapped his coat around himself and set out to comply with Neil's order when a book fell from one of his pocket. They both stared at it in horror. There on the floor; lay Neil's last copy of Tales of Witchcraft" by William Wallace."

"It's a good read," the man blurted out "but I never got to the end of –"

"No, bloody no" said Neil scooping the book from the carpet floor. "Just keep going and don't look back."

Mark Rice

Crossing to new shores

I was angry, in a festering frustrated way for years.

Waves welling up from the deep,

but as quickly as it came, it seeped away,

in my acceptance, that at least I had known him,

it was my pleasure.

I was on my own when I travelled away that day.

Friends and family thought I was mad.

Something drew me on, pushing me, driving me.

I had put an ugly hacking knife in the bag, for safety.

I was prepared, ready for what life would present

And what beauties I was shown,

what jewels were presented to me, shinier than any I had ever seen.

Now I'm holding on to a concrete life that I've built,

Tightly surrounding myself with a structured scaffold,

socially, financially, emotionally.

I'm not sure I will ever let go like that again,

I'd like to, but deep down,

the loss is aeons and aeons in my minute cells.

There's only a letting go in my imagination, looking out
now on the rolling hills.

I'm well aware that if I cement the floors too tight,

there will be no movement,

no shaking,

no crossing to new shores.

Mairead de Bhal

"This is a St Patrick's Day like no other…

In years to come, let them say of us, when things were at their worst, we were at our best…

we are asking people to come together as a nation by staying apart from each other."

An Taoiseach (Prime Minister) Leo Varadkar 17th March 2020

The Traveller

"Good to be back?" asked Judy. It had been a year and Judy was surprised by how much she had missed her eldest daughter.

"Yeah, Mum" Siobhan smiled weakly. She'd been up since five and was now flagging badly. They walked together, largely in silence through Dublin airport until Judy could contain it no more. She dropped the rucksack and turned to give Siobhan an emotional hug.

"What's done is done. You are here now safe and well and that's all that matters," said Judy wiping away a stray curl from her daughter's forehead and a tear from her own eye. "Let's give it another go, will we?"

Siobhan nodded her head. She was too tired to talk. However, it wasn't long before cross words were exchanged because the next day Judy discovered her cosmetics lying open and used on Siobhan's bed and confronted her daughter about it.

"Will I have to put a lock on my bedroom door?" she asked of Siobhan. "You will not, from now on, enter my bedroom, OK?" said Judy.

She returned to her bedroom and grudgingly hid her beloved cosmetics in her sock drawer. She secretly wished that she'd had a son as apparently, they only wreck your house, not your head

The next morning Judy visited the bedrooms gathering whites for a wash and when she returned to the kitchen, she found her purse lying open with twenty euro missing. She'd left Siobhan sitting at that table barely twenty minutes ago. "Just you wait until your father gets home!" she shouted to an empty house. She really would have to accept the fact that she was destined never to get along with her youngest daughter.

Judy was peeling potatoes an hour later when her phone rang. She dried her hands, put down the peeler and picked it up. It was her mother ringing her to say that she'd heard from Siobhan. She would be coming by coach to stay with her in Wexford today.

"So that's the plan," said Judy. She told her mother about the row and the missing money. "Now don't you let her get away with stuff while she is staying with you" warned Judy. "Mum, lock your valuables away. I'm serious; don't leave anything lying about because she can't be trusted."

"Don't you worry love," said Granny. "I'll keep a good eye on her" and in the background, Judy heard a doorbell ring. "Look - I must go," said Granny. "My meals-on-wheels lady is at the door!" With that, she was gone.

Later that afternoon Granny drove to Gorey town and parked next to the coach stop. It was raining heavily but the bus arrived on time. Siobhan was the first off, stepping onto the pavement and avoiding the puddles. She looked up and Granny flashed her cars headlamps. Siobhan was with her in seconds and deposited her rucksack on the back seat.

"Good to see you, Gran," said Siobhan and she leaned over the gear stick to plant a kiss on the old woman's cheek. They travelled back to BallyTubber engaged in conversation. Siobhan poured out stories from her time abroad and then watched Granny's face for her reaction. Granny was pleased that she seemed to have a way into the young girl's life, something her mother clearly lacked and she encouraged Siobhan on with timely "oohs" and "aahs".

The family in Dublin were delighted that Granny had company and all was going well with Siobhan apparently on her best behaviour. Granny reported daily to Judy when Siobhan went for walks and the first week passed quickly.

"She cooked for Mum last night," said Judy to her husband over dinner later that week. He almost dropped his fork in astonishment.

"My my" he uttered, "That is a surprise. Maybe she really is changing. You know, maturing."

"If so, it's about time if that is the case," Judy replied, her view still jaundiced from her recent clash with the girl. "She needs to get a job" she added.

As March progressed, the national news channel filled with stories of a virus. Covid-19 was coming and no one knew how to slow it down or to stop the spread.

"Wash your hands" was the cry of a nation but it sounded a trivial act in the face of a tsunami of pain.

"Didn't Siobhan visit Italy?" asked Judy upon hearing the news that night. Her husband instantly followed her line of thought.

"You mean has Siobhan possibly carried the virus to Granny Brown?" he elaborated. "Aye, she did visit Italy. Wasn't she there for Christmas? Remember? We rang her on Christmas day and she was visiting Venice and St. Paul's square to meet someone," he answered with a growing smile.

"Oh, thank God you're right Matthew" replied Judy dispensing with that worry in record time. The virus hadn't reached Europe much less Italy back then.

The next day we had Ireland's first fatality attributed to the virus. By the end of March, the Government instructed all to stay at home. It was now a matter of the whole country staying where they were which meant the Dubliners stayed in Dublin and Siobhan must stay with Granny indefinitely.

Judy rang Siobhan that night but found her mobile no longer worked. It looked as if she had run out of credit.

Judy rang Granny who was surprised, as she'd been giving Siobhan a fiver a week to top it up. "From what I see she slips the credit on and it's gone in no time at all. It doesn't seem to last a day!" said Granny.

"Who does she ring Mum? It's not me or her father and that's for sure!" observed Judy. "And then she borrows your phone I suppose?" Granny's silence confirmed Judy's suspicions. "You'll have to watch that Mum. You really will," warned Judy. As the weeks went by Judy grew more anxious about the situation in Wexford. Granny's initial reassuring calls telling them that she was happy, well-fed and feeling good stopped and Judy's calls to her Mum went to answer-phone more times than not.

Siobhan's phone no longer worked and now it was she who answered Granny's mobile. "Can you pass me over to my Mum?" said Judy in exasperation after she'd spent two minutes talking to her monosyllabic daughter.

"Grans asleep now" answered Siobhan stretching her sentences to her furthest limit.

"It's gone ten in the morning" commented a worried Judy looking at her watch. "Will you do us a favour and nip upstairs and see how she is?" Judy heard an exasperated sigh at the other end and then waited in silence.

Finally, Granny's voice came on the line. "How are you Judy my love?" asked Mum.

"Fine Mum, what are you doing in bed at this time in the morning?" asked Judy.

Oh, I'm fine Judy. I just felt jaded last night and decided to lay-on in bed listening to the radio this morning. I'll be up soon I promise" Mum assured her.

"No rush Mum. I'm just glad you are well," said Judy. "Have you been out at all Mum? Do you know you can walk up to two kilometres from the house? And have you seen another living soul since this started, Siobhan excluded?" asked Judy.

"I'm most certainly getting my daily walk in; don't you worry about that. I met Amy, you know my neighbour, yesterday and she's making plastic visors for the HSE now. Using something called a 3-D printer," said, Mum.

"That's great news Mum. Are you sure you are OK with Siobhan staying on with you?" checked Judy.

"She's fine" Granny assured her.

With the whole family at home, Judy was busier than ever. Somehow, Granny slipped off Judy's radar and though she thought of her daily, she didn't call that often. The knowledge that Siobhan would probably pick up the call first was now a dampener to the exercise.

Then one Wednesday night she realised she hadn't called Mum at all that week so she rang later than normal at 9:00 pm. The phone rang for ages before it was finally answered. "Ello" came a deep foreign male voice. Judy was startled and promptly checked that she hadn't misdialled. Shockingly she found that she hadn't.

This was Mum's phone. Before she could respond, Siobha

n came on the line sounding breathless.

"Hello Mum" panted Siobhan "How are you?" she asked politely.

"Don't you hello me" answered Judy her voice quivering with shock and anger "Who the fuck was that?"

"Calm down Mum, calm down," said a surreally calm Siobhan. "That was Guiseppi. I met him in Italy last year and he's a really nice guy. I suppose you could say he's my boyfriend."

"What the hell is he doing answering Mum's phone and standing in her house?" asked Judy.

"Well, he couldn't stay in Italy as it's been a bloodbath over there. People are dying in the streets Mum. He caught one of the last planes out of Rome because I was really worried about him," Siobhan explained.

"My God girl, have you no worries about your Granny? This Guiseppi guy could well have the virus and you've brought it into Granny's house, the home of the most at-risk member of our family" Judy went on.

"That is so typical of you, Mum. Why can't you just be happy for me for once in your bloody life?" said Siobhan.

"NNNNNNNNNNNNNNnnnnnnnnnnnnnnn"
the call ended abruptly.

"The little bitch" steamed Judy. "She's just put the phone down on me!"

Judy rang again but the call went unanswered. Eventually, the phone was switched off and Judy gave up.

The Dublin family swiftly convened a meeting and concluded that there was little they could do about the situation in Wexford. With the country in lockdown and police checkpoints on all the motorways, there was no way for them to get to Granny. Matthew offered to try but Judy said no. It was probably too late to evict Guiseppi. He either did or did not have the virus.

Judy managed to reach her Mum on the phone the next day and she seemed well if surprised at the turn of events. A few nights earlier, she'd gone to bed about ten o'clock, after the evening news and came back downstairs for a glass of water. There she found a strange man sitting on her couch in a passionate embrace with her granddaughter.

"I didn't know where to look, Judy. I forgot all about the water and I just went back upstairs to bed. They hadn't spotted me and I didn't want to embarrass Siobhan."

"Mum really! This is your house," said Judy exasperated with her mother.

"Now I had a few quiet words the next day with Siobhan and she apologised to me and asked if he could stay until the pandemic is over. I hummed and hawed but eventually said "yes" the old woman replied.

Judy put the phone down and wondered if that's what old age does to people? Knocks the edges off them and makes them soft. The old Mum would never have let Judy away with such behaviour.

As the days passed, the pandemic news nationally worsened but in the county of Wexford, the numbers of infections seemed to be stabilising. It was a week later that Judy got a call from Amy, Granny's neighbour.

"Hi, Amy how's things? Raining in Wexford?" asked Judy, the phone pinned to her ear as she hung out the washing on her line in Dublin. "I'm fine Amy, and you and yours? Isn't that virus an awful thing? Almost twenty thousand infected and a thousand dead. What's it like in Wexford now? One hundred and fifty-one infected eh? You lot are getting off lightly down there in the sunny South East. Yes, it must be the country air, eh?" Judy spoke nervously, hardly letting Amy have an opportunity to speak. But in her head, she knew Amy had rung for a reason. For a moment, Judy thought she might be able to stall any bad news by talking rapidly and blocking it out. Finally, Judy drew breath and Amy took her chance.

"I met Siobhan and that man outside your Mum's house this morning. They were waiting for the ambulance. It arrived while we were chatting, socially distanced you know. I'm sorry to tell you but your Mum is now in Wexford General Hospital with a suspected case of Covid-19" said Amy.

Judy's heart sunk and she felt as if she'd been shot in the stomach. She crumbled under the news and dropped to her knees, her clothing basket and wooden pegs scattered on the neat lawn.

"Well, I appreciate the call, Amy," Judy heard herself saying. "I truly do but I must go now."

"Your Mum is a fighter Judy and she'll pull through" Amy was trying to put a positive spin on it. "She was well enough to give me a wave as they took her out on a stretcher so she's got plenty of fight left in her," she added.

"I'll be in touch" were Judy's final words.

She composed herself and called Matthew who was locked away upstairs working online. They agreed he should ring the hospital and see what was what.

It started to rain in Dublin and Judy could see the first drops hitting her window pane but she no longer cared about the washing. Matthew returned saying that Granny was doing well.

She had been admitted and was in a sideward for those suspected of having the virus. That was where she was when Judy eventually managed to speak with her. "God love her," said Judy "I could hear her struggling for breath but she kept insisting I was not to worry."

Overnight Granny was diagnosed with the virus and was moved into a Covid ward where she rallied strongly before suddenly taking a turn for the worse. Her next move was into Intensive Care and being placed on a ventilator.

The doctors told Judy she fought the good fight but nothing had worked for her. They speculated that she had a particularly virulent version of the virus.

She wasn't allowed visitors even at the end so none of the family knew her final words nor could comfort her in her dying moments. Judy was guilt-ridden and traumatised by the experience.

Siobhan and Guisippi both tested positive for the virus and were housebound for the next fourteen days. They were mildly ill and Amy, that ever-helpful neighbour, dropped food on their doorstep to keep them going during that period of isolation.

None of the family could make Granny's funeral in Kilmuckridge as they weren't allowed by law to travel from Dublin to attend. Siobhan and Guisippi couldn't attend either as they were self-isolating. The undertakers live-streamed the funeral service to the grief-stricken family who watched on in silence.

Two weeks later with the lockdown still in place, a letter landed on Judy's hall carpet and she opened it. It was from Fagan's Solicitors alerting her to the fact that Granny had not died "intestate", as was previously thought. No, a will had been drawn up in the final fortnight before her death and had been posted to the practice.

In it, Granny Brown had left "all her worldly possessions to Siobhan, her caring granddaughter who had been of invaluable assistance to her."

The signature had been verified as that of Mrs Brown and the will had been witnessed by a "Guisippi Conte". Siobhan had instructed them that the house was to be sold and all proceeds along with any other assets forwarded to her at a withheld address in Italy.

"I am contacting you," wrote the solicitor "as you were the executor of your father's will and may have some knowledge of what other banks, credit union or saving accounts Mrs Brown may have had."

Mark Rice

"Unprecedented actions" to respond to an "unprecedented emergency"

Leo Varadkar, An Taoiseach (Prime Minister) 25th March 2020

Lockdown

Joe ended every section with "wash your hands",

Conversations included lockdown or exit plans.

Many counted cases, others deaths,

Internet meetings got on our wick.

Two floppy haired leaders both east and west

seemed not to care about death.

We judged, watching with pain,

Some rule breaking, some near insane,

Bridge or monopoly became the thing,

online options checked out again.

Some took to baking or cleared out the junk,

Homebound, drank or ate to cope with the funk.

Inspired some danced, cycled, or walked.

others gained fitness and trimmed down a lot.

Relationships stretched, some broken,

some healed,

 some hardly coping, some revealed.

A few went to the office, most worked at home,

fearing being broke again, another slump.

The sun shone most days and helped us a bit

other days the cold wind really hit.

We slept for longer in beds and in bunks

as weeks slowly turned into months.

I built a vegetable patch, I painted and toiled,

I watched Netflix, banged my head against walls.

I thought of doing knitting, then crochet or art,

I even took the broken sewing machine apart.

I metered out phone calls to one every day,

To another human being with nothing to say.

Like prisoners, we prayed watching our way.

Walked in fresh air for a short while each day.

Lesley Smith

"Start by doing what's necessary, then do what's possible, and suddenly you are doing the impossible."

Francis of Assisi, Catholic saint

Visiting the village

Neighbours had been shopping for them but Nora hadn't wanted to burden them with a large shop, so it had just been a few essentials each time they offered - milk, bread, fresh vegetables and a bottle of whiskey. The latter made her sound like an alcoholic but the shopping trips on their behalf were few and far between. The alcohol numbed her boredom as another evening of nothing on the telly approached.

Nora had explored shopping online and at first thought that supermarkets only delivered online shopping to people living in the suburbs of local towns. That was until one of their delivery vans nearly ran her over as she walked along her own country lane. She picked up the phone and checked out the free delivery for the over sixty-fives in this rural area even though, technically she wasn't yet sixty-five.

Though she rang a Dublin phone number she got a countrywoman on the line and when Nora came clean, as she could never lie, and said that she wouldn't be sixty-five for another six months, the woman said "Aren't you lucky because it's November here in Galway right now!" and proceeded to set her up on the scheme. So that sorted them out for the food and drink.

However, her husband's dole payment was another matter, as was the petrol needed for the lawnmower and the paint needed for the bleached decking plus the compost needed for her baby plants. As the days passed, the list grew longer and the urgency grew to exit their two-kilometre safe zone and pick up supplies themselves. The longer the pandemic lockdown went on the more fearful they both became of what danger lurked beyond their comfort zone. What was awaiting them sitting invisibly on door handles, loaves of bread, and bottles of milk or just hanging in the air waiting to be breathed in by a human?

The need finally overcame the fear and Nora drove them down to the village. She ran through her plan in her mind as she drove. He'd need to get out and fill the containers with petrol having first wiped the petrol pump hose handle with an anti-bacterial wipe. Brendan knew what was expected of him and he'd already donned a pair of disposable gloves. Nora dispensed wisdom and drove simultaneously. He's a good man but he has, at times, the memory of a goldfish. Let's go through it one more time sweet Jesus.

"Now you have the gloves on do not touch your face and do not return to this car with the gloves. Put them in the bin outside the supermarket when you are done with them. So it's getting your dole first, then over to Tom's Hardware to collect and settle for the petrol. Finally, get the other stuff. I'll have the hand sanitizer ready on your return to the car."

"You have your shopping list?" she asked. He fumbled in his old jacket returning with the crumpled list in his hand. "Good man, good man. Now put it safely away and remember which pocket you put it in,"

"And you have your bank card with you?" Another search of the pockets by Brendan ensued, which eventually ended with the card brandished for her to see.

"Try to keep the bill under fifty euro so you can tap it and avoid touching the keypad at all," she advised. He nodded. He sensed the tension in the car and was eager to defuse it. Staying silent and agreeable seemed a sensible approach to take. He earnestly hoped he would remember all the instructions.

They drove into the village and sought out the bottle bank to offload the bags of bottles that filled the car's back seats. They found a set of six banks overflowing with bottles and cans. It seems the council's collections were viewed as non-essential services. Their glass passengers would be travelling home with them today.

Back across the village, they drove until Nora indicated a turn left and she parked alongside the closed hairdressers. There they ran through their plan one more time before they stepped out of the car. If he thought, he was being trusted to complete the mission alone he was sorely mistaken.

The petrol & diesel pumps were in the forecourt of Tom's Hardware, with the Post Office set behind them. Just beyond them were the village supermarket and public house. Brendan was relieved to find the Post Office devoid of customers. He pushed open the door and nervously approached the counter. Jill cheerfully greeted him and acted as if this was just another day. How could she be so relaxed? He kept to the plan and managed to collect the cash without incident. Nora, outside gazed through the window watching his every move. She stood ready to sterilise him at the first sight of dangerous behaviour.

Onto the petrol pumps where he helped himself to the petrol, he needed to fill two small containers. He noted the amount on the pump and recited it to himself on the walk back to the car.

It was only when he'd returned to the car and deposited the petrol containers in the foot well that he noticed he'd torn one of his gloves. His bare thumb lay revealed with the torn glove fabric dangling around it. He glanced around. Nora hadn't spotted it. Brendan wondered whether to tell her? She'd go into a state of shock considering the multiple possibilities of infection around the oil-covered pump equipment handled by so many others. If he said nothing and he had picked up the virus he could pass it to her killing her. He wanted to slip a bit of sanitiser onto the thumb or put on a new pair of gloves but that would mean letting her know he'd torn the glove. Christ knows she worried enough as it is. This could tip her over the top!

He made a decision and pulled the fabric back into place and joined the queue of socially distanced customers outside Tom's Hardware. No one was allowed inside the shop anymore. Finally, it was his turn and as he moved forward he probably breached the two-metre distance rule when passing the departing shopper.

The counter stood a mere foot inside the shop and a large clear plastic screen separated him from Deirdre, Tom's wife and her team of young hardware assistants.

He found the list in his pocket and pulling it out began to work his way through it, under the watchful eyes of Nora. Lord, don't let me make a mistake he prayed. Let everything on the list be in stock too. Today he was not in luck.

Deirdre had no cabin paint. A four-way discussion then started up with the woman queued behind him, his wife stood to his left, himself and Deirdre. It appeared that no one in the local area wasted money on the expensive tins of wood paint. Oh no, they use masonry paint on wooden decks. On walls and fences too said that woman and everyone nodded. Sure, it's got almost magical qualities he began to believe. "Anyway, we don't have the Tonseal paint in stock," informed Deirdre so after due consideration and consultation with Nora who gave the local favourite a thumbs down gesture Brendan decided to buy nothing at all.

The other items on his list were in stock and his bill was finally totted up. It came to ...... 50 euro and 40 cents. He'd have to touch the keypad!

Nora watched on as his hand reached across the counter and stretched under the plastic screen to enter the four digits and hit the green button. He could see his hand shaking with the stress and it was all he could do to focus his finger on depressing the correct numbers but right now, his memory struggled to recall what four digits they were and their correct sequence. It had been weeks since they'd last shopped. Was it 4756 or 4576 or 4657 or even 7456? He now realised that he should have scribbled them on his arm before they left.

Mother of God help me, he prayed silently. OK, OK steady yourself. Use the first one that came into your head, 4756, that sounds very familiar. He'd repeated it several times and it did indeed sound like the one he should use. He began to relax. Then he thought 4657 also sounds familiar. Now don't do this to yourself. Don't muddy the water. Just go with 4756. He noticed Deidre looking impatiently at him; her arm still extended holding the card reader in front of her. I'm going with 4756 he said to himself.

"Is that your final answer" his consciousness asked of him "or do you want to phone a friend?" Now is not a time for humour he warned his consciousness. Leave me alone! He keyed the numbers in one at a time and pressed the green button. There was a pregnant pause before the machine gave its verdict. With a grunting noise, it spluttered into life and spewed forth a paper chain of receipts.

Deidre handed him the receipt and he thrust it in his pocket and glanced at Nora for approval. He got the nod. She'd be washing all their clothes when they got home and he'd incinerate the receipt later.

Then came the bad news. The young assistant whispered something in Deidre's ear and she called him back to the counter. "It appears I've sold you three bags of compost I don't have."

Another discussion ensued and Nora settled on two bags of another supplier of compost and Deirdre beckoned Brendan forward. Suddenly she reached out her hand and he automatically opened his and into it, she placed a single euro coin for the price difference in the compost.

He looked down in horror at the coin now nestling in the soft centre palm of his right hand. If it had been a lump of burning hot coal that just hopped out of the fire grate, he couldn't have welcomed it less. It was as if she'd passed to him the virus itself so unwelcome was the coin now resting on his bare skin as the torn glove had now failed him completely.

He nodded to her while his brain whirled away, filled with indecision, trying to choose the correct option because there was always a correct option.

Though not religious he whispered a prayer as he stuffed the euro coin in his trouser pocket and glanced for approval from Nora. Had he done right? She looked on expressionless. He'd know when they'd got home. Maybe she'd been as flummoxed by the turn of events as he. He managed to mumble some thanks to Deirdre and moved hastily away from the counter.

The young shop assistant carried the two heavy bags of compost out of the shop and he stored them in their car boot. Brendan walked to the nearby supermarket bin and carefully removed the gloves turning them inside out in the process. He chucked them towards the bin but some glove fingers got caught on the corner of the lid! Brendan had to touch them again before seeing them drop inside the bin.

With his nerves now torn to shreds, he returned to the car where Nora waited, armed with anti-bacterial soap and a fresh wet wipe in each hand. He wiped down both hands while singing "Happy Birthday" three times, as she was a stickler for the rules. If the government guidelines said, it was so, then so it was. With him scrubbed clean, they both sat back exhausted in their car seats. They'd barely been in the village for seven minutes but it had felt like a lifetime. Home and further weeks of isolation now beckoned and they welcomed it with open arms.

Mark Rice

*"Not all superheroes wear capes ....
Some wear scrubs and gowns."*

*Leo Varadkar An Taoiseach (Prime
Minister) March 2020*

Too soon

I am dog-tired, weary and I am getting scared.

Jim keeps looking at me when he thinks I am not watching. He looks worried but every time I acknowledge him, he says the same thing. "You will be fine, you might have to go into the hospital for oxygen or something but you will have twenty-four-hour care. It will be for the best love, let's trust the doctors they know what they are doing." But do they?

It is a new virus and everyone keeps talking about ventilators. I am convinced I will never get home if I end up in hospital. I don't want to die. I'm afraid, every time I take a deep breath or talk too much the hacking cough starts, I can't catch my breath, I can't stop the coughing. Jim had an old codeine cough mixture which I thought might help but it did nothing other than make me even more exhausted.

He keeps watching me and I keep watching him. He should not be in the same house, never mind the same room as me, we both know it. He says, "If I am going to get it I probably already have it, we are always together."

The waiting is hard. He drove me to the test centre two days ago. I wanted them to test both of us but they said the protocol only allowed for those with symptoms to be tested. The test was horrible, made me breathless, and caused a coughing fit. They stuck an enormous swab up my nose and into the back of my throat. I nearly threw up. Now we wait. I have been sick five days now. At first, I thought I was having hot flushes but somewhere in the back of my mind, I wondered.

We can't go anywhere but then who can? It's like we are stuck in our own nightmare, waiting, worrying, checking temperatures all the time, watching.

I am not religious, I don't even know if God exists but I am praying to something, someone. "If we both survive this," I say, "things must change, we are both overweight, high cholesterol and high blood pressure. They say the fatter you are the more at risk you are." When he said in his accusing way "I don't understand how you would have got it, were you not washing your hands and keeping your distance?" I keep telling myself that he doesn't mean it but it's like, he's accusing me or suggesting my own carelessness has made me sick. I don't want him to be sick, I love him, but I resent the fact that it's me not him.

We never asked how we would get the result. He gave them all the details for the form, he was the well one. They were not happy that we were both in the car and that neither of us wore a mask but what was I supposed to do. I never learned to drive so he had to drive me. He should have listened to what they said about the results but typical of him, he didn't really listen and I was too busy trying to stop coughing.

The sweating is hard, I feel constantly dirty and I suspect smell. I insist we sleep in different rooms but we keep the doors open in case I need to call him. I cannot shout without coughing. I slept a little while last night but woke with the heat, the bed wet with sweat. I took too much Panadol yesterday in an effort to keep the temperature down and the headaches away. He'd be mad if he knew but I felt it was worth the risk.

The phone rings in the hall. I listen intently, willing myself not to cough in case I miss a word. He seems to just be saying yes to everything he's asked. He says, "I understand. Yes, she will be ready." I drew in a deep scared breath then and coughed for five minutes. When I looked up he stood there with shining moist eyes and said "They are sending an ambulance. I will get some things ready for you to bring, should we call the girls?"

"Time enough when we know where we stand", I say.

~~~~~~

"Day eleven" the nurse says and I think to myself I no longer know how long I've been here in this room. I was upset when I realised that Jim couldn't come to the hospital with me. It is the longest time that we have been apart since we met, when I was seventeen, apart from that time I went on that cruise with my sister.

I would give anything now just be able to see his face or hold his hand. I worry how he is coping; we are an old-fashioned couple; he doesn't really shop or cook.

I assume the girls will have him sorted somehow but he will be aimless, lonely and helpless at home.

They let one of the girls in to see me but only for ten minutes. She was in a gown with gloves, a mask and a visor. She found it hard to hear me because I wasn't allowed to take the oxygen mask off. I struggled to hear her through the mask. I wondered how they decided which one would come in. I realised and then felt guilty that I was glad it was her, my eldest, the younger one would have been far too emotional. Debbie was more matter of fact and stoic. She ran through all she was doing for her Dad and said that I was doing okay. "Stay positive Mum, and do what they tell you".

I wasn't positive, I could see the shock in her eyes, I knew I had lost weight, lost energy and I could see the oxygen level on the monitor going down slowly even with the oxygen mask on. "Sorry", I said, taking my time, trying to breath "Look after your sister and your Dad, I love you".

When the nurse had the time and I felt, able, we had a video call and I got to see the faces of my loved ones and hear their voices as if they were at the end of a tunnel far away. I could not speak much by then but I tried to send them love with my eyes.

~~~~~~~~

I knew it was time before the doctor said so.

Although terrified at the thought I welcomed the news that I would be sedated. They would put a tube in my throat and attach me to a ventilator. The nurse said it would let me rest and the ventilator would breathe for me. I craved the rest, an end to the coughing, and some oblivion I hoped.

They contacted Jim and the girls and told them and they did a quick video call so that they could see me before the tube was put in. "Stay brave Mum, it's for the best, you will be able to rest, you will be fine."

Jim could barely speak and I could see in his eyes that he was begging me to live, not to leave him. I am trying, I thought, I am trying.

~~~~~~~~~

Jim rang every day at the same time. He knew the nurses by name. They were all kind and soft spoken but there was a weariness in their voices. He supposed that he had to remember that I was one of too many patients, now lying face down on my bed head dipped lower than feet with the tube attached to the ventilator.

When I lightened a little, I thought how I would love darkness, quietness, and some way to move unaided to stretch my sore limbs.

Occasionally I would feel human gloved hands turn me or manipulate something. Some spoke to me while they worked but most seemed automated, exhausted, disconnected. I never saw their faces.

Time was blurred by now; I didn't know day from night, the lights were always on. Every now and then, a sharp pain roused me despite the sedation. A needle being poked in my arm, an electrode being pushed into my chest.

Once they seemed to wean me off the drugs and I woke. I was on my back then and was struggling to breathe; I panicked, had they done something wrong, why were they standing there watching me, why were they not helping? Then someone injected something into the tube and I slept again.

A nurse used my phone and did a video call with Jim and the girls, she was kind to him but he was crying. He never cries, he is as I said an old-fashioned man. "She is not suffering," the nurse told him. "She has just no longer got the ability to fight anymore, her kidneys have shut down and she is not responding to anything we have tried. It is only a matter of time."

He asked her to hold the phone close to my ear. She did and somewhere, somehow I heard him say, "thank you, my love, I will be with you soon, I love you so much. The girls love you. No need to fight anymore, rest now."

Lesley Smith

Anticipation

She sat on the bench in the park. It was a cool wet day, with that driving rain that creeps in around the edges and makes everything damp, even reaching those places covered and protected and considered safe.

The park was quiet. Who wants to walk in the rain? There were a few, the running enthusiast whose internal need for an adrenaline rush pushed him out the door, running shoes, shorts, a 'North Face' jacket, nothing on his head. The weary mother pushing the pram, trying to keep an eye on the youngster scooting up and down the path.

Amanda shivered a little. She had a hat and an umbrella and the wind was soft but still, she felt despair.

Derek had not promised. He had said he would do his best. He really wanted to see her, told her he longed to hug her, spend a day with her, even to just see her face and talk in the flesh.

She had not seen him for months. They had never gone this long before without getting the chance to be with each other.

Living alone during lockdown gave her too much time to think, too much time to miss him. She had been watching updates on the talk shows, couples on zoom talking about having more time together than they ever had, baking together, overeating, ordering take away, drinking. She would love to experience that with him.

Amanda had not even known where the park was until today. She had used Google maps to find it. This is his neighbourhood not hers. Usually she avoided this area, easier to ignore something you do not see.

He had said that he could not be out for long especially now with nearly everything closed. He would have to say he was walking to the local shop for something and hope no one wanted to come along.

She thought she saw someone come through the gate but realised she imagined it.

He had said around 4pm and it was 4.15pm now. She had been sitting on the bench for nearly an hour, just in case.

They had talked for a good while the other night. He was sitting in his car running the engine to keep the battery charged. He said that things were okay, he was working from home, taking up the dinner table while his wife worked at the kitchen table. He said it was hard for everyone with the kids there all day, bored missing their friends, insisting on being entertained. He said the only peace was when the kids went to bed.

Amanda asked him what they did then and he said, "You know the usual, food, a few drinks, a chat, a zoom call or quiz with friends, occasionally a film." He had sounded cheerful when he said that and a surge of jealousy and fear had welled up inside her. It didn't sound like the unloving mistake of a marriage he had described but then these were strange times.

Getting restless now, Amanda wondered where the shop was. Standing she walked slowly around the edge of the field, the cold now piercing her bones, she hugged herself to get warm.

Then she noticed a small group across the playing field on the other side of the park, a man, a woman and two kids came into view. The couple were holding hands and chatting. Every now and then, the man broke away, ran, caught and threw the rugby ball back to the kids, returning in between to catch the woman's hand.

Looking around her, Amanda watched the family approach. Her eyes widened with surprise as she saw that it was Derek. They passed close by, far enough for social distancing close enough to speak but she just stared. He mouthed sorry and bit his lip.

She watched them leave and then walked back to her car, tears in her eyes.

Lesley Smith

A sentence with no end date

She stared out the steamed misty window. Rain fell in vertical sheets on the car, a wash of greyness, where the mere outline of Flanagans was just visible.

Peggy had been there for two hours, parked across the road, frozen, except for her breath, which rested in condensation on the inside of the glass. The drips running down the inside of the car testament to her being alive.

She didn't move, just sat there, occasionally when there was a lift in the skies, making out the shop door and the occasional customer who had braved the storm.

Not her, no she couldn't brave the storm, not now, not ever, she grimaced. It wasn't any physical pain from sitting in the car for so long, but it was heart pain that welled up and died down, and at times over the last week, had made her breathless, gagging to be alive. It could come on her at any time, day and night.

She had been looking forward to the state holiday the next day and had gone into Flanagans to buy bacon and cabbage.

Peggy loved the tradition of the Saints day, the green flags; the friendly bumbly parade down the main street, the children all festived out in their Irish dancing costumes, shivering in the predictable cold North Wind.

The floats scarce on imagination but colourful in bunting; the vintage tractors driven with pride and smoke; the new articulated trucks brought by Brady's - slick in their international allure, and Thelma's hairdressing salon with all the pretend clients getting their hair done on the Mc Namee's trailer. And the local band, blaring out led by old Gerry Mc Intyre on his trumpet.

She hadn't noticed any difference, that day she entered the shop. Going over it in her mind, again, and again, how was it that she had not picked up on the gossip long before Agnes stopped at the deli, and grabbed her by the elbow

"Hey Peggy," she whispered. "Michael is gone." "What do you mean?" she asked. "Michael is gone, left, up and disappeared. He has been seeing that young Polish waitress in Caffolas, and he's away with her to Dublin. Left the family home, left Maria and the kids, left them all, just left a note, and said he was sorry."

Her heart lurched, she had nearly fallen behind into the dried foods section, Agnes steadied her. They had been friends since national school, when she, Agnes and Michael were the only children in 3rd class.

Always together, the three musketeers Master McGibbons called them. They climbed trees, hunted for crabs, made paper aeroplanes, always up to mischief. At twelve, her feelings changed.

Michael had changed too. He had grown taller, taller than she had. She had to look up at him to talk to him, his hair longer, dark and curly. His face had filled out, and his square jawbone made him thoughtful and handsome.

When she was around him, she began to blush, to stutter, she couldn't stop thinking about him, dreaming about him. It all surprised her. A school girl crush. It was during the summer, and they were hanging out together more often, since school had closed.

Peggy had nonchalantly checked out if Agnes felt the same about him, but at that stage she was meeting Johno.

They had all been swinging on a rope across the river that day. Agnes and Johno, herself and Michael.

It was windy, even more exciting than usual. When you jumped off from the edge, you went out to the middle of the river, and then swung back with such whistling speed, your breath was taken out of you.

They laughed and squealed at the fastness of the return. When it was Peggy's turn, she remembered smiling at Michael, he had pushed her back, and the feel of his hand against her shoulder, made her flesh burn.

She flew through the air, and threw her head back to look at the sky. She was happier and freer than she ever was. Up and up she flew, above the houses and the farms. She could just about see her home, and her poor mother trying to make ends meet, her father out as usual, not coming home till late expecting his dinner. Up above the fighting and the arguing , the shouts and screams.

Then an awful snap, the rope, which had been tied for years, gave way. She fell, quickly, rushing like rubbish down a chute, into the water below, her leg hit something sharp and bounced her into deeper waters.

She was bobbing up and down screaming, Michael waded in and fished her out. The last thing she remembered was his eyes looking down at her, and she managed a smile.

The doctors said she would always have a limp. The rock had severed her tendon. Apart from that deep scar, she would survive. She couldn't ever ride a bike properly, couldn't dance, couldn't wear high heels -but all else was perfect, the doctor said. She had turned her face away.

Returning home, she regained her strength but the drag of her left leg slowed her down, for the rest of her life.

She went on to secondary school, and struggled through teenage years determined to make a go of it.

That was the type she was, her teachers said, works hard and makes the best of it. She only met her grief, outside of school, at the local dance. There Peggy clung to the back wall; her inability to move gracefully displayed her crushing handicap for all to see. She stopped going after a humiliating night, when she glanced over to see two girls laughing at her.

Michael never asked her to dance, never twirled her around the floor, never took her outside. He did with others. He was a regular. She was not surprised when he got married suddenly to Thelma's daughter and had a baby son a few months after.

At night over the years, she remembered him, searching for conkers in Murphy's glen; fishing of the rocks in Mullack; looking for frogs in Lannigans field. Most of all she remembered his hand on her shoulder, and his eyes looking down at her that fateful afternoon.

Peggy prayed for him, for them, but in the end she'd resigned herself. She would wait, she would wait for him, and if they were destined for each other, she would be ready and willing. She loved him.

He had two children, Edward and Tracey, she watched his tired wife pushing them around the town in a buggy or holding their hands, as they crossed the road. She always looked harassed. Peggy always lowered her eyes when she passed them, not wanting to lock eyes with her.

Michael had come into the post office over the years, they had talked, but nothing lasting, he was friendly, but clipped. Always in a hurry, he never lingered. She held onto the counter for minutes after he left, trembling like a leaf while trying to maintain a composed smile for the next one in line. Now he was gone, disappeared to Dublin with a Polish lady.

That day in the shop something shattered inside her. She collapsed into herself, it was like her innards had melted and her bones sunk into her body. Her eyes shrunk into her head, she couldn't talk, couldn't go out, couldn't bring herself to work.

Her parents were gone now, and had left the house to her. Here she stayed, with food delivered, and she slept, occasionally dressing, but living on tea and digestives.

Without Michael she was nothing; he had kept her going all these years; the idea of him; the occasional sight of him, the thought that somehow against all odds they would be together. She knew it was mad, but what could she do, this was how it was.

She didn't know why she had got up this morning, started the car, and drove down to the main street, just to sit.

Others had seen her over the last week, pointing and whispering. But she didn't question herself anymore, she hadn't the energy, and frankly she didn't know what she would do in the evening, tomorrow, or next week, she had no idea.

Her boss had rung, and told her the job was gone, she couldn't keep it open any longer for her, with no sick note, no explanation She was sorry, she had said and maybe when she was feeling better, she might be able to give her a few hours.

Peggy grabbed a digestive from the glove department.

This was the best she could do. And maybe just maybe she'd catch a glimpse of him and know, he'd come home. She'd settle for that.

Mairead de Bhal

"It is amazing what you can accomplish if you do not care who gets the credit."

Harry S. Truman, 33rd US President

The Lockdown Runner

When Paddy failed to get over a football injury four years ago, he took up running. When the Park Run started in a local park Paddy realised he'd found his calling.

The concept of the park run is a five-kilometre run or walk for people of all ages. From ages, nine to ninety, the participants came alone, or in couples or family groups with children or with dogs. The participant's times and placing are recorded at the end of the run and posted on the Park Run website later that day. All the runners previously completed runs are also saved on the site.

Paddy realised that this was exactly what he'd been seeking all his life. Hundreds of people to compete against who were not themselves super fit. Most Saturdays he'd attend and run not only to beat his own personal best time but to compete and beat similar-aged runners.

Over several months, he enjoyed the running and began to recognise the runners in his age group. Once over the finish line they sat gathering their breath outside the cafe and chatted amiably. When Paddy started running the park runs he felt sure that none saw the race the way that he did, that they were just trying to beat their own personal best times and not trying to beat him or the other runners.

However, he soon discovered he was not alone in treating the leisurely non-competitive jog in the park as nothing short of a full-scale Olympic qualifier. There were many more "Paddys" in this world and some took great satisfaction in beating him to the line. Some egged him on during the race when they'd pass him labouring up a hill. They'd say words like "Press the Button Paddy" to which he'd heartily reply "I haven't a feckin button to press!" Similarly, he loved that last hundred yards when people eased up with the line in sight and he found another gear to sprint past them. Oh yes, there was psychological warfare going on out there! If the guy in front of you was an eighty-three-year-old asthmatic with dodgy knees he was still fair play for overtaking on the run-in.

Now, with the pandemic, the park run was a thing of the past. Self-isolation was only a few days old when he went exploring the apps on his mobile phone and found one which counted his steps. It offered him the chance to join a weekly 100k step competition which ended at midnight on Sunday. With only ten competitors and instant updates, once you synced your step counting watch with your mobile phone, your cumulative steps for the week was updated. You then improved a place or two in the ranking but all the time aware that the other nine had step counts to update. Paddy loved the idea and began investigating his opponents gleaning what he could from their profile on his app. They came from all over the world and the group of ten people changed weekly though one or two seemed to appear frequently in his group.

Having stumbled on the step challenge competition he found himself leading the list on that first Saturday night. Paddy was confident of holding the position the next day as he ran ten kilometres and took a walk on the beach with the dog. Indeed, through the day, his lead lengthened and his confidence grew. So much so that he didn't bother to check the leaderboard on Sunday night. He sat relaxed, feet up watching television and breastfeeding a beer.

He got a rude awakening on Monday morning when the app emailed him notifying him he'd finished ....second. Paddy raced to open the app and found a leader board, which only repeated the shocking news. He'd been caught in the closing hours by a certain "Ronny" who to that day had propped up the foot of the table. Ronny had suddenly walked thirty thousand steps late on Sunday night. He had been caught napping and knew it.

The following week he set off like a man possessed and walked increasing distances as the week progressed. He led the table from day one and increased his lead daily. Sunday arrived and Paddy awoke to find the heavens had opened on the small village he lived in. It rained solidly all day. Paddy ran up and down the stairs a few times but his step count remained stubbornly low. As the hours passed Paddy's lead was whittled down to only five thousand steps from his nearest challenger and fifteen thousand steps better than Ronny, who looked to have not walked a step since Friday. He lurked menacingly in the tenth position.

"The sneaky sod," thought Paddy "he's not syncing his steps with the app for days on end and then he is connecting late on Sunday to win the challenge. Well, two can play that game me boyo!"

Paddy stepped onto his cross trainer in his sitting room and watched an entire Gaelic Football match from 1968. He yanked away vigorously with his arms and strode manfully up and down with his legs on the contraption for the whole match. Eighty minutes later, he tottered off the appliance and checked his watch. He was appalled to find only three thousand steps recorded. Feck. A country lane walk of eighty minutes would have yielded at least ten thousand steps. He collapsed onto the couch and towelled himself down. The sweat was running down his back, he was a spent force.

Tired and dejected he checked the leader board and gained comfort that Ronny was still loitering at the bottom of the table. Others had closed the margin of his lead despite his best efforts and now he only led by two thousand steps. Outside the rain continued to bounce off the driveway and he knew he'd struggle to add the steps he needed to assure victory.

It was an hour later that his long-suffering wife first heard some banging and crashing coming from the hallway. Opening the door she found her husband struggling to carry his lateral thigh trainer down the stairs and into the sitting room. He assured her he was fine and didn't need a hand so she left him to it.

Paddy stepped on board this rarely used appliance and a test run revealed it was counting his steps much better than the cross-trainer. So off he went spending another hour moving laterally left and laterally right but going nowhere. Having watched two episodes of Gardeners World he stepped off the machine and checked his steps for the day. He now had over fifteen thousand steps and he held them back, for now.

He showered for the second time before tea that night and felt refreshed and confident. By 8:00 pm most competitors had made their move and he was in second place to a woman called JoJo. He itched to post his stored steps but resisted.

At 10:00 pm he was fourth but knew his stored steps would sweep him to victory. Ronny still lay in the doldrums at the foot of the table and hadn't added a step in two days.

By 11:00 pm with bed beckoning Paddy synced and his steps propelled him to number one. Ronny was still holding back. Paddy was worried.

With ten minutes to midnight, Paddy rolled over in the bed and under cover of a duvet; he checked the apps leader board. His phone illuminated the whole bed and the white linen sheet he'd slept under now resembled a brightly lit circus tent. "Feckin Hell…." Ronny had synced and he was now number one! Paddy calculated the difference. He trailed Ronny by almost five hundred steps. Silently he slid out of bed and in his pyjamas crept downstairs into the kitchen. Outside the rain continued to hammer against the windows and puddles of water covered the patio.

He had eight minutes to clock up five hundred steps. Buttons, his dog sat in his bed peering intently at his master. Paddy looked at the dog and suddenly it came to him! He had a plan that just might work. Strapping his tracker watch to the dog's collar he walked Buttons to the back door and whispered "Squirrels" to the animal pointing him towards the furthest corner of the garden. Into the black darkness, Buttons bounded, barking wildly as he went. Paddy stood by awaiting the animals return and watching the minutes pass.

Dog and watch were back with two minutes to spare and Paddy could afford the luxury of half a dozen laps of the kitchen before syncing. He checked the leader board as midnight arrived. He'd done it! "See you, Mister Ronny!"

Exhausted he returned to bed where a bemused woman sat waiting for him. "And what was all that about?" she asked but then she had second thoughts and dimmed the bedside lamp. "Oh don't bother love I've taken a sleeping tablet. You can tell me about it in the morning." "Night night love" "Night night darling"

Mark Rice

"Remember that sometimes not getting what you want is a wonderful stroke of luck."

Dalai Lama

Filling a void

Hands across a chasm

the wish to fill, to substitute, to rebuild.

Drive on

but, all is changed the intent unknown or undesired,

still, recognising a void I reach across,

first technologically with simple words, throwaway phases,

then by phone, strange unmet voices.

Distant deafening in fear and anticipation, dread.

Then to the first sight, first meeting,

boxes being ticked, unticked

queried photos, wrinkled older face, teeth not white,

clothes grubby, an old shirt.

Judging being judged, wondering what next

where might it go, where should it go?

Thoughts of other options, other profiles,

weariness but still maybe not too bad,

beggars not choosers at this age and size,

Forced unreal but real of this time.

I hate it. A fabricated way to move on

a slim slight chance of magic,

possible frogs to meet,

Kiss, no not to kiss, with Covid.

Talk of sex, too early too scary.

In the background guilt that I am doing this

reduced to a weird unnatural way to meet,

not touch, a solution to being lost, alone.

Lesley Smith

The Power of Prayer

He'd attended services every Sunday and sat there now in their usual row. He glanced around the empty church. The ten o'clock morning service was late to start and he could afford a little reminiscing.

He remembered when there was only standing room for the latecomers at midnight mass in this church. They stood or leaned against the grey concrete walls or formed lines in front of the wooden confessional boxes. They stood for an hour or more as the service moved slowly through the stages, punctuated by choral interruptions and lengthy readings.

The lot of a latecomer was the constant changing of weight. Shifting from one foot and then to the other, rising up on their tiptoes to powering down on their heels. Then there was fidgeting in pockets, noisily blowing noses or whispered giddy conversations behind cupped hands. All of which only served to provoke the wrath of an old biddy who glared back at them. For the two young lads, the mass seemed to last an eternity.

The priest, old Father Barry, aware that he'd got a huge audience of rarely seen souls took full advantage of their reluctant presence. He'd give a long rambling lecture on the wrongs of modern society. The drinking in excess of alcohol, the menace of taking drugs and the evergreen chestnut, the evil of fornication. For a man who professed never to have participated in any of these vices he sure knew a lot about them. He'd speak on and

on, so long that from twenty minutes into the service
there was a constant procession of men, stepping up
onto the altar to genuflect and make their urgent ways to
the toilet. Not surprising considering they'd been
lowering pints for hours before joining the faithful. Their
presence was largely down to the churches ruling that if
they attended the midnight mass on Christmas Eve it
excused them from church attendance on Christmas
Day. That was when mass pulled in enormous crowds of
faithful believers. Father Barry only ever stopped when
the cacophony of coughs, moans and nose blowing
threatened to drown him out completely. That or he lost
his train of thought, which was often.

This church could hold three thousand souls and
often did back then. Now it was restricted to holding
fifty.

He wondered what made the priest late today.
Father Mbuto Salabi, a kindly young man from Nigeria
was here now because of the work of missionaries
Ireland and the Catholic Church had dispatched to
darkest Africa in the last century.

He knelt now and said a small prayer for Marie
and his parents all beyond pain now. He thought of each
one and looked ruefully at his mother's favourite seat in
the second row, third in. He could close his eyes now
and see her sitting there, her shoulder-length curly black
hair, her black reading glasses, and her lips moving in
time with the prayers. Eventually, Tom pulled his old
bony arthritic knees off the padded kneeler and checked
his watch again today. Ten past ten it showed and he still

was alone. He sighed and wondered whether to leave the church now or stay a little longer?

Gazing around he spotted, near the front of the altar, a metal table where row upon row of empty candleholders stood. Below them hung, a box that contained candles and another that held donations made by the laity. As it happened, Tom had a two-euro coin in his coat pocket. A coin that had sat there for months since the lockdown had begun. It was now something he had no use for. He paid electronically everywhere, tapping his card as he went. No one dares to use cash.

Tom walked down the central aisle and approached the candle stand. Just beside it stood a small table containing a roll of paper towelling and a bottle of hand sanitiser. He slipped the two-euro coin in the donation box and heard it fall noisily to the floor of an empty tin box and roll along before falling silent. The metallic sound echoed around the vast building.

Seeing the sanitiser Tom realised he'd walked past one at the entrance to the church. He'd been so focused on picking up the service sheet he'd clean forgotten to wash his hands. So he poured a large blob of the blue liquid sanitiser into the palm of his right hand and worked it well into both hands, front and back, thumbs and fingers.

He reached into the other metal box and retrieved three tall white wax candles and placed them upright into holders next to each other on the top row of the stand. "Bless you all," he said to himself "You never had a pandemic to survive but you faced many other challenges in your time. Miss you, my love."

Nearby lay a box of matches and he took one out and struck its red swollen head against the rough side of the box. The match flared up with a brilliant bright flame that lit up the church.

Tom stretched out his arm to light the three candles and had managed the first two with ease. For the third candle, he needed to stand on his tip-toes to reach the wick and as he did so he was hit by a blast of intense heat from the area of the candles. The third candle had lit but so had his right hand and lower arm. They were engulfed by a ball of flames. He smelt the smell of burning flesh and hair.

The alcohol in the sanitiser had ignited with a flame, which had jumped from the candles as his arm stretched over them. Damn. In a moment he realised he'd have to keep his left hand away or it would ignite too!

Tom leapt backwards like a startled gazelle and stumbled banging the back of his head on the first row of wooden benches. Helplessly he waved his burning arm about but the flames just grew higher, now being fanned by his frantic actions. The pain drove him to scream out loud. He could see the paper towel he thought he could use to smother the flames with but it was several feet away and on top of a table. He was still lying on the tiled floor in front of the marble altar and Tom knew he had to do something fast.

Before Tom could pull himself upright he was hit from behind by a wave of cold water. It dealt him a glancing blow before travelling on to douse the flames on his hand. The water hissed gently upon impact with his damaged hand, before rolling down and forming a pool on the tiled floor. Tom's saturated hair dripped water into his eyes and blurred his vision. Startled, he found Father Mbuto Salabi standing beside him and grinning, in his hand an empty bowl.

"I was on my way in when I heard your cry," Mbuto explained. "I desperately looked around for something to help you with and well, the Lord provided." "Provided how?" said Tom a bit slow on the uptake. "You were saved by water Tom" chuckled the priest "Holy Water."

"Come with me, I have a medical kit in my room. We'll sort you out," said the priest helping Tom to his feet and being careful to avoid touching his hands. "You may still need to take a trip to the hospital. You're looking, how would you say, a bit raw in places."

"Thank you father," said Tom meekly as they walked together towards the back of the church.

"It all happened so fast" mumbled Tom and then he added, "You know I don't believe in all the church teachings?" He scanned Father Mbuto Salabi's face for a reaction.

"I've not met many that do Tom," said Father Mbuto Salabi "but maybe this shows you that as long as He believes in you and watches over you, maybe that's all that matters."

Mark Rice

*"Do not judge me by my success.
Judge me by how many times I fell
down and got back up again."*

Nelson Mandela

The new door

The new door is on the office, swinging smoothly,

no scraping of the wooden floor.

Honey brown pine, with a clear window to the inside bright sunny space.

A nature rug of oranges and yellows beckons

soft green cushioned armchairs lend an air of comfort and luxury.

There are no customers.

No business.

Do I hang on

Or do I let go.

Let go of a business,

Built over long years of travelling and working late,

Squeezing in my other lives and loved ones around it.

Exhausted, but the opportunity to pay the bills, the surety of having enough,

The main draw,

Do I hang on,

Or do I let go.

When is it the time to say goodbye?

Adieu to a part of life that has taken its toll,

Business cards, letter headed notepaper,

Telephone calls, diaries,

Sweat, tears, dark hours, gulped soggy sandwiches and cold coffee,

Affording status and meaning to the week.

Nobody calling now.

All postponed indefinitely.

The message on the answer phone says 'closed for the foreseeable future'.

No bookings coming in.

Debts starting, bills piling,

The bank manager will be calling.

Do I walk away or stay.

Walk away from my new door

Will I float or bounce off the bottom.

Disappear into a drain,

Who will I be?

A sad old lady looking into windows of a past life,

Or an elder adventurer heading out afresh,

You get what you wish for, they say.

Do I hang on or do I let go.

Mairead de Bhal

The circus is back in town

I knew better than to interrupt the grown-ups especially when my grandmother and my mother were whispering together in the kitchen while my grandfather sat in the sitting room waiting for his tea. We were often asked to keep an eye on grandad and to come running in to warn them if he was coming through to the kitchen.

I don't remember what age I was but I was small when I first heard the word circus. I had seen pictures in a highly coloured book that belonged to my older brother, pictures of elephants, clowns, trapeze artists in beautiful costumes. Everything happened in a tall red and white striped tent.

"The circus is back in town," I heard my grandmother say one day. I looked up, eyes wide, full of hope and expectation. I had never been to the circus, but now, maybe I could go.

When my brothers and I were eating our 'egg in a cup' at teatime, I chatted away and asked Mum and Dad if we could go to the circus.

"The next time they come to Dublin we'll see what we can do." Dad said. "They only come once every couple of years and so we never know when they might be here."

"Are they not here now, Dad?" I asked. "No love, I don't think so," he said. I looked expectantly to my Mum but she said nothing. I was so disappointed but I supposed they had their reasons.

Months later, I heard the same phrase from my Grandmother "The circus is back in town".

"Just as well," Mum said. "At least you will be well cared for and have some peace over Christmas this year."

As I got older, my Grandmother often mentioned that the circus was back in town but we never went.

Years afterward, I realised that talk of a circus being back in town was coded talk between the two women. "The circus is back in town" was code for when my grandfather was seeing and spending time with his mistress. Whilst this might seem to be a strange thing for the two women to appear to celebrate, I realise now that it signalled a safe quiet time with no shouting, no violence and the start of a period of generosity of spirit and caring within my grandparents' marriage.

My grandfather was in a good mood when his mistress was around. Afterward he would treat my grandmother really well. It never lasted and his alternate persona always reappeared bringing fear, anxiety and physical harm.

Lockdown caused an increase in domestic violence. I wondered how my grandmother would have coped, unable to have her daily visit to her daughter's house, stuck in a house with a man who had little patience and whose hands used to demonstrate bad humour and frustration. There would have been no 'circus' possible. Would the occasional twisted arm, blackened eye have become broken bones or worse. I shivered at the thought.

My friend Leona and her husband had relocated back to Ireland from Toronto. I had last seen her here in person two years before, at their wedding and was heartbroken to have her leave to go to live in Canada but she was home in Ireland now. We talked on the phone from time to time, which was lovely.

In May, I got a video call from Leona. I was delighted, as we had not seen each other since she had been home.

We chatted about the usual topics, the boredom, the concern, and the cases. I told her I was lonely and commented on how lucky she was to have her husband John. I could see him behind her on the sofa watching something on TV. We talked about how we were doing the shopping and baking and she asked me for my recipe for banana bread.

"John loves it," she said "and that's what prompted me to ring you. I knew you would be able to help me. I remembered you had a tried and tested recipe".

"Sure," I said, "do you have a pen to write it down?"

"Yes, she said go ahead". I saw her glancing behind her and then she did something strange. She held her hand at chest level facing me, opened her palm as if saying no. She folded in her thumb and then closed her fingers over it making a closed fist. While doing this she stared at me, eyes glassy and guarded. Then she scribbled fast while I went through the recipe.

"I will try it and hope for the best, you never know when you start things how they will work out" she said.

"Here's hoping, thanks, I knew I could rely on you, you have never let me down".

"I will ring you next time," I said. "Look after yourself".

I ended the call and sat there wondering. I replayed that call repeatedly in my mind. Her eyes seemed to be pleading, that strange thing she did with her hand. The somehow forced good mood.

What to do? I rang a nursing friend and asked her what she thought. I described the actions Leona had made with her hand wondering if it meant anything.

"Oh no," she said. "I saw that on Dr Phil months ago, it is a way of letting someone know that you are in danger without speaking."

I think I already knew that before my friend confirmed it. There was something in Leona's eyes.

The weight of responsibility was heavy on me. I had to act but I was afraid despite everything that I had misunderstood. What if there was nothing wrong?

I rang the women's aid helpline. They asked me if there was any way that I could talk to someone in her family or contact Leona and arrange to meet for a walk or pick her up something in the shop to leave at the door and get a chance for a quick chat. They suggested that I phone her and ask her questions that she could answer yes or no to so that she could confirm what was going on without raising any concerns to anyone who might be listening. I did not know and was afraid, both of being wrong and if right of making something worse.

I sent her a text, breezy and chatty. "How did the banana bread go? I will be in Pearse Park at lunchtime today and tomorrow for my daily walk. I would love the human contact even at a distance if you are free and can meet up for a short while."

"Can't promise but will hope to see you. Banana bread worked okay," Leona, replied.

That day I waited anxiously from about midday to two o'clock but she did not show. I was stressed all night afraid and wondering if I had done the right thing. I was concerned that I may have made a bad situation worse.

I went back to the park the next day and with great relief saw that she was there. She looked sheepish, pale, tired but she smiled. We could not get close or hug but we walked with a good distance between us.

We made small talk and chatted about everything apart from her signal and her safety for the first ten minutes. Eventually I stopped walking, turned to her and said. "Sorry but is everything okay at home? I am only asking because I thought you were giving me a signal on the phone the other day".

She looked at me embarrassed. "I know," she said, "sorry, we were having a tense day and I got it into my head that John might lose his temper and hit me. I was scared. I think it is the whole situation with this virus. He has a bit of a temper and being on furlough and stuck at home doesn't help. He'd never raise a hand to me."

"Sorry about that. I was not even sure you would have realised and had hoped you had not."

"Has he ever lost his temper and hurt you before?" I asked worriedly. "No not really," she said. "There was just one time when I drove him mad, nagging him about bills and things. I was totally in the wrong and he snapped. He was really sorry about it and actually cried afterward. He didn't mean it and I should have known better. It was my fault."

"Are you sure", I asked, doubtful.

"Of course," she said, "anyhow I better get back soon."

We walked on a little while longer and then she said she had to go.

"Great to see you."

"You too," I said, really wanting to hug her. I watched her leave.

Weeks later, I heard she had tripped and broken a tooth and cut her face. They said she had an almighty bruise. Friends said she has been clumsy and accident prone since she came back from Canada.

I know that signal was a call for help at that moment. I wonder if there is ever a time in her life when the circus comes into town for Leona and she can totally relax and not be on guard.

I think of how my grandmother had begged my mother when she was dying to look after her Thomas. She has said that he would be lost without her.

Sometimes we wish we had done more or acted sooner.

Lesley Smith

The signal for help is a one-handed hand gesture women can use to alert the person they are talking to that, they feel threatened. The signal involves holding your hand up with your thumb tucked into your palm, and then folding your fingers down and trapping your thumb in your fingers. It originated in Canada as part of the Canadian Women's Foundation.

"Language has created the word 'loneliness' to express the pain of being alone. And it has created the word 'solitude' to express the glory of being alone."

Paul Tillich

La petite mort

Leona had to scratch that itch she was feeling. Amid the Coronavirus here she was trying to figure out a solution. Everyone is worrying about Covid rules, wearing a mask, not wearing a mask, leaving cert results. All I can think about is sex, Leona thought.

Am I weird she wondered? I'd love to ask other people but how could I and whom would I ask? It is not even as if I have been having sex, it is going on for six years now since I have.

I was not ready before this and I know that. I honestly never felt a stir of desire for five out of those last six years but something has changed in me and I don't know what.

Maybe my head just cleared a little or my heart is mended a little. Maybe it is because I am a bit fitter.

I remember looking at that man in the gym just before lockdown, he was panting and groaning lifting weights. Very annoying to imagine what he must sound like having sex I thought to myself. Disgusting annoying noisy man but it stirred something in me, not a desire but a memory.

When lockdown happened life's distractions disappeared overnight, it seemed. Leona was alone with time to think. She realised that life was too short and that she didn't want to be alone.

I need a partner she told herself. Something has to change.

The jump from the thought of needing a partner to this obsessive thought of sex just happened. The last time she felt like this was when she was pregnant and craved sex to the point of obsession for a short while near her due date. Tom had laughed at her but he had not complained. In fact, he had enjoyed his sex-mad wife.

It would be hilarious if it were not so weird, Leona thought. No chance of finding a man, even if I wanted to, and even if I joined those online dating sites, and even if I found someone half-decent, with this virus we wouldn't be able to touch.

I will buy some toys on the internet, she thought, no one will ever know and it is not as if there are other options.

Leona looked online and read through advert after advert. They were expensive toys and some of them she had no idea what anyone was supposed to do with them. She had never owned anything like this and realised that there is a world out there that she has never been part of.

In the end, she ordered three items, which had great reviews; a dildo, a tube of gel and a vibrator, which they called a G spot vibrator. Leona even now in her middle age had no idea if she even had a G spot or if she had how you were supposed to find it. The bill came to

€236 - just as well she was saving a fortune on not buying clothes or eating out.

She waited three days in fear and anticipation. What if the postman knew and looked at her funny? What if it went to the wrong address? What if the boys came upon it when they were visiting?

Given that her sons were only standing at the end of the driveway when visiting, she knew this was impossible still her stomach churned at the thought of someone else knowing.

Then one afternoon she got in from her walk to find a note in the hall. Sorry, we missed you, package in the green bin. She rushed out and retrieved a harmless looking package from the bin.

One item needed charging before use so she plugged it in. The other one needed AAA batteries. She had not thought of batteries and was irritated that she had to get some somewhere. Even simple things like getting batteries needed thought and planning now. Then she realised that the electric toothbrush used the same batteries so she was sorted.

Leona had not been close to a man or even considered being close to a man since Tom had died. She had only wanted Tom and she missed him.

Now she found herself planning a solitary date for solitary sex. She was shocked herself with this fledgling desire for something she has not even thought about in years. This virus changed life in the oddest of ways.

I feel like a pervert, she thought, but there was a little joy in the anticipation and the knowledge of what she was planning. I know it's silly but I am going to wait until I go to bed, she thought, it seems less odd.

She had a nice dinner, nothing fancy. She opened a bottle of wine, thinking a glass or two would give her courage. Then she had a shower, washed her hair, dried it and put her best nightdress on.

Now and then she checked the lights on the charger, it turned green (fully charged) just as she went for her shower. She unplugged the vibrator, swapped the batteries from the toothbrush to the dildo, took the gel and advanced up the stairs. She felt like a naughty schoolgirl.

So into bed. She sat up and turned things on and off. Noisier than she expected. The vibrator nearly jumped off the bed when she put it down for a minute to look at the gel. The gel felt cold and didn't smell of anything, a bit glue-like. I hope I don't mess up the sheets, she thought. You would think there would be some indication on the gel about staining or not. She wondered if she should put an old towel underneath her but somehow that seems too functional so she decided to risk stains on the sheets.

Now, what are you supposed to do with what, she thought, is there an order? She put some of the gel between her legs, it was oddly cold and then warm. She held the G Spot vibrator against herself. Not exactly exciting she thought. A bit irritating and ticklish. Nevertheless, she persisted, lying back and trying to remind herself of Tom and how he looked and how it had felt to make love with him.

It was hard, electric toys no matter how expensive would never be a substitute for making love with the man she had loved all her adult life. Still thinking about him helped.

"If you are watching me now, Tom, you will be laughing I know and raising your eyes but a need is a need and you left me too early."

She was beginning to relax. It felt nice. Nice was about all she could say but still, she could feel her heart rate rising and she felt cosy and somewhat aroused.

Her face flushed and she was beginning to think that maybe this was a good idea. Her excitement was increasing and she had not even used the dildo yet. Her breathing increased and she felt like she may even get to a release of some type easy enough. She lay back moving the vibrator from left to right, eyes closed, moving into her own world.

Suddenly the phone rang.

Her heart nearly stopped with the shock - a video call from one of the boys on WhatsApp. She tried desperately to turn the vibrator off but couldn't find the off switch in her panic. She shoved the vibrator under the pillow and answered the call, hoping the buzzing wouldn't be noticed.

"How are you Mum", her son David asked. "Are you in bed already? Is everything okay, you look flushed? Are you sick? " He asked in alarm.

"No, no I am fine," Leona said realising that she was indeed breathless. "There was not much on TV so I came to bed early to read," she said.

"Are you sure Mum" David persisted.

"Absolutely," she said, "now tell me, any news."

David now reassured chatted a bit about working from home. How people were so annoying when he was out walking weaving on and off the paths avoiding people. Eventually, he said good night and the call ended.

Leona put the phone down, took a relieved breath, retrieved the vibrator and eventually got it turned off. She pulled out a tissue and wiped herself dry. The mood was well and truly gone now. She felt shocked and exhausted from the excitement, not sexual but of nearly being caught doing what she was doing by her grown up son.

She put the toys away and mused to herself. "If only he knew," she thought. More things than Covid can cause shortness of breath and flushed faces.

Leona picked up her book and opened to the page she had been reading the night before. The desire for sex now totally gone, at least for tonight.

Lesley Smith

"You yourself don't have to be shaken by mortal danger in order to feel your mortality."

Seamus Heaney

Mrs S

John watched breakfast television. It was a day when, and he glanced at his watch, he'd normally be stuck in a traffic jam on the M50. He yawned. Upstairs the kids were playing quietly with their Lego and in the backroom, Mary was already logged in and working. Wasn't he the lucky one?

John walked into the kitchen, popped two slices of bread into the toaster and hung about waiting for them to resurface. He gazed out the window, down the length of their garden and beyond it into the kitchen of their elderly neighbour. There she was now, Mrs S, and across the distance, their eyes met. He gave her a cheery wave and she returned it. "Good woman yourself" John mouthed to her. Do you know she'll be one hundred next Friday?

They'd only moved into the house when his boys kicked a football into her garden. Most people would have just handed the ball back but not Mrs S. She stepped back a foot or two, sprung up, and over the dividing wall carrying the ball tucked in under her arm. She landed, it had to be said, a little unsteadily but before he could reach out and lend her a hand she'd risen, dropped the ball to her feet, dribbled around his youngest lad and buried it in the bottom left-hand corner of the net.

At the time, he wondered if he was dreaming. That or watching a segment of Mrs Doubtfire. It was the start of what has turned out to be a wonderful relationship, especially since John and Mary had lost their own parents when they were young. Mrs S had, in essence, become a substitute grandmother for the boys.

The toaster popped but what he saw next stopped him in his tracks. Mrs S coughed. She coughed so vigorously that her shoulders shook and a startled expression came across her face. He stood transfixed looking at her and her at him. The toast was cooling in the toaster but for him, only one thing now mattered. Does she have the virus?

Now as he watched, he saw her old fingers reaching for a packet of tissues and prising one out. She blew her nose into it and then glanced again in his direction. She looked scared and he felt terrified for her. Getting it at her age would kill her.

He pulled a quizzical face and mouthed "You OK?" Mrs S had now regained her composure and wiped tears from her eyes, eyes moist behind her thick-rimmed spectacles. She smiled weakly at him and waved his interest away. "I'll be fine John," she mouthed back to him.

Reassured and much relieved he was set to turn away when a sixth sense caused him to take that extra glance. If he hadn't he wouldn't have seen a jerky downward motion of something. Mrs S was gone from the window and he couldn't be sure but he thought he'd spotted a brief wave of a hand. Not a cheery horizontal wave but a sudden dramatic frantic wave. A wave from an arm of a body that had suddenly jolted downwards. Christ almighty has she slipped and fallen in the kitchen?

"Are you eating both of those?" came a voice, inches from his ear. It was Mary now by his side and reaching to open the fridge door. She took out a jar of strawberry jam and walked to the sink grabbing a knife from the top drawer. "Yes, ...I mean no" he replied.

John couldn't take his eyes off Mrs S's kitchen window. Maybe even now she is lying on the tiled floor, passed out and bleeding.

Mary spread the jam and took the first bite of her toast wiping away a dribble of jam from her chin. "John – come on answer" she grew impatient with him. "I don't know why but I'm ravenous this morning. I'll have your slice too" she threatened. "Look I'll put two more on for you" and then Mary asked, "Has the kettle boiled?"

Mary became aware of her husband's total distraction and walked to the window where she followed his gaze. "You playing the peeping Tom with our Mrs S? Now, John, I've heard of the male attraction to the older woman but I thought our local centenarian was safe!"

"It's not that love, it's just I think she's in trouble and she may need my help."

"Tell" she demanded and in moments he brought her up to speed with the morning's events. She nodded a few times and if he thought he was going to be disbelieved, he was proved wrong.

Mary had educated herself about the virus and had developed almost an obsession with the Coronavirus Covid-19 because if she didn't, she knew she would be dead. She had what they called underlying medical conditions.

"I'll go over and check on Mrs S. You stay here and mind the kids," she announced solemnly while gazing down the garden at the still vacant window.

This had the potential to be a deadly mission and she couldn't let him go, because of the very real risk that he'd veer off plan and come back with something that would kill her.

Mary going meant Mary knew she'd be safe. She knew she'd stick to the protocol. John going meant, at best, fourteen days of uncertainty. She'd be a nervous wreck by the end of it. It had to be her.

They tried Mrs S's mobile phone one last time before she left and it rang out unanswered. Damn the woman, the mission was Go.

Mary washed and dried her hands slipping on a pair of disposable gloves. She needed a facemask but right now any in the country were in the hands of the National Health Service staff. She'd have to improvise and searched the kitchen for something suitable, Mary placed a clear glass pot lid inside a hoodie which she then pulled up and over her head. Now she pulled tightly on the hoodie strings, knotting them firmly together. Pleasingly the lid stayed in place. She peered out from behind the glass at John who was holding back a giggle while nodding his agreement with this novel facemask. Mary glared at him. "C'mon love, you must admit you look funny. Last time I saw anything resembling this was in an episode of Doctor Who!"

She'd seen this idea on Facebook during the week and loved the concept of something solid yet transparent to protect her from the infection. To complete the outfit, she donned a blue raincoat with full-length sleeves and enough length to cover her knees.

John then placed a rucksack on her back, which contained a selection of antibacterial sprays, sanitised J-clothes, clean towels and a first-aid box. She also put on a pair of plastic stretchable slip-ons over her runners.

He slipped her mobile phone in her right pocket and a headphone in her right ear with the microphone clipped to her blouse. With that, he rang her number. "I'll be with you every step of the way," he said reassuringly. Mary walked out of Sparrow Drive and around the corner and into Tangle Hill watched by John and the two boys who were glued to an upstairs window. "Dad, is Mum going to defuse a bomb or something?" asked their youngest.

"I'm going in," she updated John across the airways as she proceeded up Mrs S's driveway. She slipped past the old cream Triumph Herald that was quietly disintegrating in the driveway. Grass was growing between the wipers on the front windscreen and a passenger window lay half wound down and open to the elements this past six years. Moss had formed in the rubber surrounds of the window and Mary had seen cats sleeping on the car seats last winter.

Mary inserted their emergency key into Mrs S's front door lock and turned the key. She found herself in a narrow hallway with a staircase to the left and a door into the kitchen straight ahead. She felt nervous as she'd never been in the old woman's home before.

Her heart raced and her breathing accelerated causing the glass screen to fog up. She stopped for a moment to wipe clear the moisture on the glass with a tissue. She composed herself so that her breathing was once again regular and controlled.

Walking across the worn-out carpet, she noticed a pile of unopened post stacked high on a small wooden table and wondered how long they had been there. Just as she reached the kitchen door, she felt something touch her arm and then it ran its cold touch down the whole right side of her body. Onwards it pressed forcing itself against her and as she backed away, it followed. Mary tumbled to the floor screaming. She couldn't prevent the primeval scream that came from deep inside her but the sound was largely muffled by that fecking glass screen which clouded up again and banged on her nose as she fell sideways away from her attacker. She expected a follow-up attack but it didn't come. Everything was still and silent in the hallway.

"What's happening Mary?" John shouted deafening her in one ear. "Answer me, Mary, come on say something, anything." John was worried.

Mary lay there winded and couldn't move or speak for a full minute. She heard a crack as she went down and thought she'd broken a bone but upon examination found that she'd broken the plastic first aid box in her rucksack which had cushioned her fall.

She'd had enough of the glass visor and as she removed it she discovered she'd brushed against Mrs S's hoover which was stored in an open cloakroom cupboard in the hallway. "I'm fine John. Just a little hassle with the cloakroom. I'll tell you later."

Mary pushed open the kitchen door and stepped into the room. It was empty. "She's not here John" Mary reported. "No Mrs S, no blood, on the tiles, no ………. nothing" Mary continued. She walked around the kitchen running her fingers along the counters checking for dust, checking the fridge for out of date food and checking the freezer to see if Mrs S had supplies stored away. She had.

"Downstairs is clear. I'm going upstairs" Mary reported to John and started up the staircase. She'd only taken one upward step when she felt a hand on her shoulder. Mary stifled a scream and spun around to find Mrs S standing directly behind her with a bemused look on her face.

"Mary love, what are you up to?" Mrs S asked genuinely puzzled.

"I could ask the same of you" Mary answered, "and while I'm at it can you move back a bit further Mrs S, social distancing and all that." Mrs S obliged.

"I'm just back from my morning walk in my new runners dear" and Mrs S pointed to the white gleaming runners on her feet.

"But John thought you fell in the kitchen and you needed some help. I came to give it to you and there you weren't, you were gone!" was as much as Mary could answer.

"Oh, the pet, I did have a bit of trouble slipping these runners on in the kitchen this morning but the bunions make for a tight fit in all my footwear. Well, tell John not to worry I'm fine as you can see."

"But aren't you supposed to be cocooning and staying home?" said Mary as she picked up her glass pot lid off the carpet and stuffed it under her arm.

Mrs S smiled "I don't do cocooning love. Never did. I'd fade away if I didn't get out for a walk every day. Be off with you now and give my love to the boys."

Mary trudged home surprisingly tired for it was only 10 am.

Mark Rice

"As a nation, we have been through a shared experience and as we move forward, we will never forget what we have lost, what we have learned and what we have gained"

Leo Varadkar, An Taoiseach (Prime Minister) June 19th 2020 (Reopening)

Although

Although life different let impedance inspire.

Hold those we love.

The ebb, flow of tides,

moving, returning,

daylight into night.

Despite the fears sheltered in our minds,

hold onto every colour, shadow, shape.

Faith gives ballast from future pain.

Even in uncertainty, face the future.

Reach for connections.

Trust the light to shine,

to aid the world to smile again.

Lesley Smith

Memorial Gardens (Summer 2020)

Rich roses in circular beds, beckoning us in the sultry heat,

To smell and touch the softness bursting through dark fertile beds,

Regally displaying summer beauty,

In memory of the thousands, lost at wasted war,

Blood red and Orange, shrilling battles.

Soft pinks and whites, ebbing grief, tears and wasted dreams,

Purple and pinks, welcoming home,

Those battered and bruised

To families who bandaged and tended broken bodies.

Red gore trickled down through generations who didn't understand the carnage.

Forlorn women holding homes together,

Feeding hungry children, explaining father's absence,

soothing nightmares, and rages,

Going to bed, alone, bitter, weary,

Destroyed long after the guns and tanks had stopped and the rivers ran clear.

We breathed in and out.

We chatted and sweated,

in the hot sun,

our picnic over.

We sat on the cool stone walls discussing changing families,

planning our lives in earnest,

Stillness of the garden,

calming conversations,

Smoothing away fears, preparing us for cooler winds and an autumn of letting go.

In the late afternoon, a slight prickling of my skin.

Wake up, wake up,

In the stillness of the heat,

A slow quiet repeating melody,

Never forget; never forget, the precious life,

never forget to live, to live,

Love with your hearts, love,

Laugh, dance with abandoned joy,

Swirl around like the tendrils of a young child's curls.

March to your own tune, march,

Don't take orders, you know what's right.

It built to a crescendo,

We missed out, we missed out,

Our poor families, our dreams,

Enjoy yours; enjoy your life;

Wake up, wake up.

I shivered, as I closed the park gate,

Looking back,

I bowed to pain and sacrifice,

Hardship, bullet ridden battles of mud and terror.

I will not forget you; I will not forget you,

Young and old, rich and poor,

Lying there together.

Linking my friend, we strolled home in the evening warmth,

The smell of roses lingering behind us.

Mairead de Bhal

"There are two ways of spreading light. Be the candle — or the mirror that reflects it....."

Edith Wharton, American novelist

Covid Day

On a Covid morning I awoke to the sound of birds,

The curtain gently moving with the slight breeze at the sill,

I stretched and lay, contented in my bed,

I could see the sun had risen it's pretty little head.

On a Covid afternoon I listened to my heart,

I thought of loved ones near and far, so close yet far apart,

I watched a robin land nearby who looked me in the eye

I cried a little tear just then and gave a little sigh.

On a Covid evening I sat there all alone,

I thought of all the chores I did and what was yet to come,

I watched the day turn into night and sipped a little wine,

I wished for clinking glasses,

that simple little sound.

On a Covid bedtime, I lay my body down,

I have a little thought for those sick, those never coming home,

I said a prayer of thanks for another day that's past,

Closer to a solution. How long might Covid last?

Lesley Smith

Cuckoo

Cuckoo she shouted as she dropped the shopping bag on the counter.

"Cuckoo, here I am." He heard her faintly in the distance. He straightened his back and looked out on the horizon out past the fields, to the sea beyond.

"Cuckoo, here I am" the voice was louder and more urgent; She was advancing up the steps. "Harry, I'm here." Turning he made his way to the descending rock path. He was up at the top garden, preparing the soil for the new seeds. Slowly he took the steps one at a time. His knees were sore, it was always harder coming down.

She was already putting the cups out on the table, and the Pettits pastries were on the cake stand.

"Well," Harry said, "To what do we owe the pleasure of these," he grinned.

"Well," she said, "I know how you have a sweet tooth. You pour and I'll serve."

Even if his daughters were living here, they could not compare to her. How he had developed this friendship was beyond him. He had no friends. No one bothered about him, why would he be bothered about anyone else.

He had been hospitalised last summer. It was a turn and warranted a stay for respite in the local home.

Mary was a carer there. The daughter of an old school friend, who had died in his forties, she lived with her mother and sisters at the end of the town.

She introduced herself the first day he had arrived. Her freshness and frankness caught him by surprise. He had lived for thirty years in a cold house, with a wife that thought he was a fool and daughters who had followed their mothers' lead. Warmth was not an emotion he was used to.

She came every morning and fluffed his pillows, and straightened the bedclothes, bringing his breakfast shortly afterwards. There was always the steady banter, about the weather, the gossip and how well he was doing.

In truth, Harry didn't feel like leaving, when the matron said he was in fine form and could depart their facility.

Mary had said she would visit him, and get any shopping he wanted, it was on her way home. He knew it wasn't. She lived at the opposite end of town. He permitted it, he allowed it to happen. And so it did.

It started once a week, on a Saturday with the shopping, and then she started calling mid-week, on a Wednesday at 2 pm. She talked about the town, and what was happening with this one and that one.

He slowly felt his heart begin to thaw. He looked forward to her coming, he found himself listening to the radio and deciding on topics that he could talk to her about.

Today, she looked different. Her hair was tied back, and her blue eyes shone out from a pale face. Sturdy is what he would call her, and she was wearing blue jeans and a short cream jacket.

"I've got something to tell you," she blurted out after the first mouthful was eaten, He had noticed in the last few weeks, that there were shadows under her eyes, and sometimes he'd glance at her and there was something nervous in her disposition.

He let her relax. He took in the peaceful rural scene. He looked up, and she caught his eye, "I've something to tell you." He heard her intake of breath, "I'm pregnant," she gasped. 'I'm pregnant."

He felt the pain in his heart, like a passing dart. He nodded at her. Not saying anything.

Now it was her turn to stare out at the gentle hills in front of her. He didn't know whether to congratulate her, but it was clear that she was upset.

"Before you ask," she said, "it was a mistake. A one night stand with a neighbour." "He's not around," she explained quickly,

Again he nodded, and pushed his cap back on his head.

"I mean I like him, but, well…. he's married. His wife is Mammy's best friend for God's sake."

Now he began to think of this man and her together, and he tried to keep the thought out of his mind.

Down, down and out of his mind.

"Anyways, I can't stay at home now, I just can't start explaining to everyone what happened. I can't face the questions." She buried her head in her hands. The tears rolled down, the sobs started. "What am I to do, and I can't go back to work, I couldn't face that awl matron and her questions…"

He found her hand on the table and patted it, and managed to say, "There, there don't worry. Don't worry. You're not the first who had a baby like that in this parish. But it's changed times. Changed times."

Without lifting her head, she quietly repeated, "But where will I go, where will I stay?"

Without thinking, he turned to her and said "Why here? I have three empty bedrooms, you can take your pick. You'll be safe here, and sure you can go into town to sign on, and take some time to decide what you want to do?"

She raised her eyes first and then her head "Are you serious? Harry here, would that be okay?"

"I'm the boss, of my own home," he smiled. "And God knows I suffered for many years, to arrive at this freedom, and I'm telling you, you are welcome."

She jumped up and put her arms around him, and gave him a hug. "Oh it'll be just for a few weeks until I get myself sorted, she managed a smile."

He didn't dare ask her about whether she was keeping the baby, but she patted her tummy when she was leaving in a familiar way, that made him think that bonding had started.

She moved in the next week, arriving with her little red car filled to the brim with CD'S and plants, lamps and cushion covers.

They settled into a routine, with him working in the am, and she cooking dinner and tea, and watching TV together at night. She grew bigger and bigger.

The barber in town, asked him, about her. "People are saying she's moving in on you, and that you're the father of the baby." He smiled at the last assumption and enjoyed it. At 76 years of age, there are those who think he's up for it, that really amused him.

"Let them say what they want," he replied, "it's no one's business but mine." There were two other men, sitting beside him, and he detected an element of jealousy when he walked out, he wasn't sure. But he did know that they continued to talk about him as he walked down the street.

As she had grown bigger, she had grown more beautiful in his eyes, she walked slowly around the kitchen, with a grace that pleased him. Somehow, he couldn't remember watching his own wife in these circumstances. No memory at all, was it when he was milking 200 cows to keep all the plans for the extension paid for in full? He had a memory of sleeping out in the cow house though, to save time, so that he could be on duty there in the early hours. That went on for a whole summer.

He knew Mary had received phone calls from her family, but she took the phone into her room, and he could hear her repeat that she was not going home, that she was not going to tell and that she was getting on with her life. He wondered did she ever get phone calls from the man in question. There were two times, he heard a car come up the lane, and he thought he heard voices outside, when he looked out, he saw the white Mercedes, and he heard her slam the door, and walk inside. He never questioned her about it.

Then one sunny August morning, he heard a vehicle drive into the yard. He was pottering in the sheds looking for a rake, when he turned around he saw his two daughters step out of the shadows. Like a military operation, they spread out, and eagle-eyed looked around the outside of the house. One spotted Mary's mini.

"You have visitors" the youngest quipped.

"Hello," he said, "yes I do." He didn't move. The elder said, she'd like to have a cup of tea, after the journey from Dublin.

At this stage, Mary in blooming beauty strolled out of the house. She looked at the women and beckoned them in. He would never have allowed them in, but in they marched.

Into the spotless kitchen, with fresh flowers. They sniffed around and then the younger one said she wanted to use the bathroom. As they settled, he knew the one who had left was checking out the house, and sleeping arrangements. He knew their history and their way of thinking. He felt his bankcards in his pocket and was glad that he had placed any important documents in hiding.

Tea was made. And eventually, the one who had tripped off returned with a smug look on her face. "How come there are no photos of mother in the house?"

Harry looked at her, "I took them down the day after your mother died," he said quietly, they are in the parlour, I'd love it if you took them with you. I have no need for them."

There was a heavy silence, the girls looked at each other. "This is our home," they protested. They had not been in the house for 10 years. "This is our inheritance." They glared. He knew this was coming, he had envisaged this coming for many years. He had rehearsed it well. Mary got up to leave the table. "And who is she? What is she doing here?"

Harry turned to face them, "This is my friend, and she lives here with me. With regard to your inheritance, you will be looked after in the will, don't worry about that, but as for now, I would like you as soon as you have had your cup of tea to leave the house."

The girls heckled, but Harry managed to stand up, and with his new mobile, thrust it at them said, "I will ring the police if you don't leave in five minutes." They looked at each other, banged the cups on the table, throwing withering looks at Mary as they stormed out. He heard the screech of the BMW, as they tore away.

Mary sat down with a sigh. "Look at the trouble I've brought you," she said.

He felt a familiar dart in his heart region, and he took a seat, the inside of his body grinning, he had waited 20 years to be able to say that. As long as they were catered for in the will, that was their only worry, he knew that they would leave him alone now.

Mary screamed, she stood up and there was a pool of water on the chair beside her. "The baby," she said, "the baby is coming." He put her in the car and drove to the local hospital.

As she was being wheeled in, she grabbed his hand and said, "I'd like you to come in with me." He was taken aback, he had never seen any of his own children born, their mother had no time for that, no you stay well away from me, after doing this to me, was her call. The nurses asked for Mary's next of kin, and she nodded in his direction.

It all happened quick enough, his temperament being one of calm, allowed her to get on with the job. Her last scream, pushed her daughter out and when Harry saw the child, he knew he had to protect them both that was now his duty. He could feel it in his bones in his slow blood that trickled through his body.

No ifs or buts, this was his duty. Making her comfortable, and pushing the pillows behind her head, he watched her as she was sleeping. So peaceful with the new baby in the cot beside her, quiet. He slipped out of the room and down to the car.

Driving home, he thought about how he discovered in the last few months, money going missing from the house, not large amounts, but notes that he had from dealing a few cattle. She was taking it. He knew that. For what he wasn't sure. Was she leaving him after the baby, did she need the few bob, to plan ahead? All he knew though, was seeing the baby being born, had erased any doubt in his mind.

This baby needed to be looked after. He could help. He had set some arrangements in place with the solicitor; the will would be favourable to her. And she would be protected from the daughters. That gave him some peace, there was no redemption there.

As he drove into the yard, one of the cows poked her head out of the shed to welcome him home.

He was tired, very tired, and with the evening sun, warming the car, he turned off the engine, and sat back, he felt that familiar dart in his left arm, he put his head back to rest and a small smile rested on his face as his eyes closed.

Mairead de Bhal

"Not all wounds are visible. Walk gently in the lives of others…"

Eleanor Roosevelt First Lady of US March 4th 1993 to April 12th 1945.

Numbers

I became a Facebook troll. I started daily spats with Kevin Lennon who lives in the USA and it all started with the numbers.

Kevin called Covid-19 fake news, a Democratic Party plot, scaremongering and nothing more than the flu. He quoted the number of flu deaths in the USA annually and wrote that Covid-19 was no big deal because it would not even kill that many. He quoted figures: numbers of tests, numbers of cases, number of deaths, per state, per capita, per county, per city you name it. I disputed some of the numbers and the accuracy of sources – I was told the sources I quoted were all lying and that the sources he quoted were all true. When I asked him the method of collection and how accuracy was checked he told me I was an "asshole" who shouldn't be discussing the USA as I was not American. My opinion didn't matter.

I felt I was hitting my head off a brick wall.

I was also at that time, seeking information and trying to do good by sharing what I felt was important to share. I was sucked into the 'a friend of mine who is a doctor in Italy,' 'my brother in law's sister's friend is a patient in ICU and is sharing what it feels like,' 'a prominent doctor in France who is also a member of government.' It took me and a lot like me to realise that these were often created and fictitious characters.

Even trusted friends were sharing information that was untrue.

I looked to the official numbers from the HSE and/or the WHO. I soon discovered that the "truth" was often only part of the story, that often we were comparing apples and oranges.

People told me we were doing really well in Ireland. I looked for the per capita numbers and realised that we weren't doing well at all given our population and our geography.

Everyone talked about the R number (reproduction rate, the rating on a disease's ability to spread) and getting the R number below 1. The R number was like the weather as if today was a good weather or a bad weather day.

We compared how many miles of kilometres we each walked each day, how much weaving in and out we did.

Straight line walking went out of fashion so we talked about step count.

We waited each night for the count, number of new cases, number of deaths, number of ICU admissions, number of ventilated patients, number of available beds, available ICU beds. The amount of Personal Protective Equipment that was needed, ordered, delivered.

We watched the scales in both the kitchen and the bathroom. We discussed how much weight we were putting on and how much flour we had left to cook the next batch of scones. The Covid stone became real. How many rolls of toilet paper we each had or admitted to buying.

People compared stories of loss or having beaten the virus. How many days they were in the hospital, in ICU. How many were allowed at the funeral.

The numbers kept coming – how many stupid things President Trump said, how many attended the protests, how many attended the rallies, how many registered for the tickets. How many days in the presidency, how many days to the next American election.

How many days since our election and still no government!

I became obsessed with numbers and expected to see them floating in the air. Slowly I realised that trolling on Facebook was a coping mechanism for me. I couldn't scream at the virus or blame anyone in particular for this reality so I took my anger and venom out on Kevin, at least, for a while.

I have stopped now, a little calmer, a little kinder and more understanding, or at least for the moment.

I say for the moment because I am counting – counting and watching the deaths in the United States rising.

Am I waiting to tell Kevin that he can relax now when they reach 700,000 deaths. He had told me that

that was the expected death rate if every American got the virus because there was a very low death versus infection rate. I really wanted to scream at him that day for being callous and appearing not to care but vengeance and the ability to reply smartly in the future is too beguiling to waste so I bide my time.

I am ashamed to see what I have become.

Now everyone talks about numbers of clusters, numbers of flights, and numbers of masks. We are counting lost jobs, closed firms, takeaways per week, time allowed in the restaurant and in the pubs. We worry about those who have committed suicide, those who are dying from cancer and other illnesses because of delays and lack of services.

It's all numbers – from hours of sleep, to tomatoes successfully grown.

The coronavirus which appeared in 2019 started all this.

It will end.

Perhaps the USA's flaming numbers will result in them reaching herd immunity before the rest of the world. If indeed herd immunity is possible and it is proven that you acquire immunity by, having it and are protected from getting it again.

Some Americans seem willing to spend their lives like pennies but they may actually gain the dollars back faster than we think.

Who knows maybe Kevin Lennon will post something to put me in my box and prove that it was all scaremongering and a hoax. I hope so.

In the meantime, I keep watching the numbers and the months passing on the calendar as I count the time to the next flight or holiday. I hope that I will not be counting deaths or sickness amongst those I love while I wait.

Lesley Smith

"Even as the winter comes in, there is hope. And there is light. ...

Having given it that careful thought, the Government has decided that the evidence of a potentially grave situation arising in the weeks ahead is now too strong. Therefore, for a period of six weeks from midnight on Wednesday night, the whole country will move to Level 5 of the Framework for Living with Covid-19"

An Taoiseach (Prime minister)
Micheál Martin 19th October 2020

Cancel Christmas?

Lewis was in his room playing with his little brother
Fionn. He sometimes wished he could be playing with
his own school friends but visitors are not allowed to
come to the house now. Fionn was five, two years
younger than Lewis. He was okay to play with and Lewis
liked his little brother most of the time but it was not the
same as playing with his friend Matthew. His Mum told
him that he could not go to his friend's house or have
him come over to theirs because of a virus. That was all
the way back in March just before St. Patrick's Day when
the schools had been closed and the parades had been
cancelled.

Lewis had not really understood what a virus was
but he knew it had flown over in a plane from China.
His best friend Matthew was a little older. Matthew
explained it to him on their first Zoom call. "It's like an
invisible tiny enemy that no one can see but it is
everywhere," Matthew has said knowingly, "it lands on
your hands and goes through your nose and mouth into
your lungs and makes you sick and if you get it you
might die." Lewis was scared when he heard that.

His Mum has said that it was nothing for children
to worry about and that we just had to keep Granny safe
and wash their hands.

He understood better though when Matthew
went on to say "we do not have to worry because the
virus is friendly to children and does not attack us. It

only uses us to bring it from place to place. That's why you can't see your Granny and I can't go fishing with Gramps or have him come over to work on the tree house." Matthew had looked really sad then but Lewis was not sure if it was because he could not see his Gramps or because the tree house was not being built. His Gramps had only just started it when they had to stay home and no one could visit. Lockdown was what they called it and all the adults had to stay home from work.

They had had great plans for using the tree house as a fort during summer. Matthew had told him that he and his Gramps had tested the WiFi signal at the end of the garden and they were going to be able to bring their tablets and play games out there. His Gramps had even looked at bringing an electricity supply out so they could plug them in. The first thing they had done was to make the ladder and tack it to the trunk of the big tree. They had finished the first circular platform around the tree but that was as far as it had gotten and Matthew's Dad had said he was not to go up that ladder to the platform as it was not safe yet.

Lewis had not been in Matthew's house since March, which seemed to him an awfully long time ago. Lewis liked Matthews Gramps he was able to do woodwork. Sometimes he let Hugh and Matthew use his tools while he supervised them as he had saws and sharp knives in his toolbox along with screws and drill bits.

Lewis was able to see Matthew in school now and at GAA practice and that was great but it would have been even better if Matthew could come over to hang out in the house now and then as well.

They were lucky as they were in the same pod in school. There were eight kids in their pod and although one boy, Mark, annoyed them sometimes, they all got along.

This year school was different. They had to go straight to their classroom when they arrived in the morning, last year they had played for a while in the school ground while their mums and the odd dad chatted and then their teacher would come out and make them line up and go in together. Hugh did not really mind going straight in, better than being at home.

The parents all wore masks and so did their teacher Miss Valerie. Miss Valerie had told them that she had many masks because her mother ran them up on her sewing machine. She had one that had a Liverpool emblem on it (bit like a dragon) that was red, he liked that one best, especially because he and Matthew supported Liverpool football club.

This year was different and some things had been a bit disappointing but what was worrying him now was that he had heard someone on the television say that if something did not change then this year Christmas might be cancelled. He might have paid no attention and not really have believed it but tomorrow is Halloween and Mum said they could not go out trick or treating this year. Lewis had wanted to go from door to door getting sweets and scaring people in his costume but they were back in Lockdown again.

Lewis and Alex wore their costumes to school last Wednesday and he had felt great dressed up as a green swamp wizard. He had rubber spiders, snakes and gung on his wizards robe and had a big scary mask.

Alex just wore a Spiderman suit which was not really scary at all but he wanted to wear it and he is only five and Lewis supposed with his painted face it looked okay.

Lewis's Mum has painted his face as well so he could take off the mask and still look the part. His Mum and a few of the other mothers had dressed up as well. His Mum had a purple wig and a witch's mask and wore a long black coat. She did not really look scary but she made him and Fionn laugh and run away when she tried to scare them by making cackling noises and chasing them around the house.

Lewis had worn his costume to Taekwondo as well but that was not the same as trick and treat. His Mum said that they were going to have a couple of friends over to the backyard to play some games together and that they could dress up and they might be lucky and get some goody bags. They were going to do bod for the apple and Mum was making chocolate apples as well. He was okay with that once he knew Matthew was coming over but Christmas worried him.

His Mum came into his room and told them that their tea would be ready in twenty minutes. He could smell something baking and hoped it was his favourite banana bread. He thought about asking his Mum about Christmas but was afraid in case it was true.

Lewis was thinking just that when she turned and asked, "Well what is that glum looking face all about?" Lewis was a bit startled. "Is everything okay? You are not fretting over trick or treat are you? I explained we were going to do things differently this year."

Fionn kept playing with his cars and just ignored his Mum but Lewis smiled and said "No Mum I get it and I am looking forward to Matthew being here."

"Then what?" she asked.

Lewis considered for a minute and then decided he would ask about Christmas and presents in a roundabout way.

"Mum what will happen if we are still in Lockdown for Christmas?"

He was about to ask about Santa when she cut in and said "Now Hugh that is a long way off yet but don't worry we will be spending Christmas in your Granny's as usual and your aunt, uncle and two cousins will come over so we will be together don't you worry."

"But Mum," Lewis blurted out "what about Santa? Is the North Pole on the green list?"

His Mum was a bit taken aback that Lewis was even aware of a green list but then she smiled and looked at him a bit teary eyed and anxious, "Oh I have been so busy that I forgot to show you, Santa sent a message to my phone for all the boys and girls in the world. I meant to read it to you. I will show you after tea don't worry, mostly good news, I can smell the cake. I better go down and check it", she said heading for the stairs "Come straight down when I call you, ok."

Lewis sat there intrigued and a little bit relieved. Good news his Mum has said. Still he needed to see what Santa had said. He never knew that Santa sent message or even had a mobile phone and in fact had never considered the possibility but then he supposed most grownups seemed to have one so why not Santa.

It might be easier to message him on his Mum's phone with his list instead of writing a letter longhand and posting it, he thought, but Lewis did not think his Mum would let him use her phone for that and he was too young to have one himself. After a few minutes, his Mum called and both Lewis and Fionn rushed down to eat their tea of pizza and chips, followed by milk and banana bread.

They had finished their tea and had just finished their baths before their Dad got in from the office. Lewis had liked it better when both his Mum and Dad had been working from home. The sun had been shining most days and he liked when they took a break and went either for a walk or on their bikes or scooters. He had played ball with his Dad in the park while his Mum had minded Fionn. He was a bit young for football and got tired quickly.

Lewis had not liked having to play quietly at home all the time so that his Mum and Dad could get some work done though and sometimes he and Fionn were bored. Lewis was usually well behaved but Fionn had not understood work or why his Mum and Dad would not spend their time playing with him. They had missed school and playschool. Fionn had had a few tantrums and one day he had seen his Mum cry after one of them. She seemed a bit stressed and tired and he heard her whispering to her Dad one day something about Granny but he could not hear what.

Lewis was anxious, he had heard that old people were getting sick and dying so he did not like it when his Mum or Dad were not at home and even though he talked to Granny on Zoom nearly every day he worried about her. He did not say anything but sometimes he woke up at night and could not get back to sleep for thinking about it.

Some of the boys in school had started talking about people fighting about masks, he did not understand why but he hoped no one would fight with his Mum when they went to the shops.

Dad played with Fionn and him for a while and promised to read them a bedtime story but Lewis just wanted to know what Santa had said. He saw his Dad looking at his Mum when he asked. Mum said she would read it for them but that he should not be thinking of Christmas in October really.

"Just the same I suppose given that this year is a bit different it might be a good idea to write your letters for Santa early."

"But is he coming?" Hugh asked hesitantly. "Is Christmas cancelled?" He added quietly.

His Mum and Dad looked at his pale concerned face. "Oh Lewis of course Christmas has not been cancelled, what gave you that idea? It might be a bit quieter and we will not be visiting friends or going to see Santa in the shopping centre but of course we will have a Christmas," Mum said. "We are going to go to see Santa at a drive through so that both Santa and we can be socially distanced and safe."

"Hold on now and I will read Santa's message," she said picking him up and sitting on the couch, phone in hand and Lewis on her knee. Fionn sat beside them on his Dad's knee and asked his Dad was Santa coming tonight. His Dad hugged him and said "you have to wait lots of sleeps before Santa comes but Mummy says Santa sent her a message so let's listen to what he said."

Mum opened her phone and started reading. "Dear boys and girls, I hear some of you are worried that I might not make it to your home this year because of the Covid virus. Please do not worry I have been in contact with every country in the world and I have been given clearance to fly in and land as normal. I will have to stay home for a few weeks when I get back to the North Pole to quarantine but I always need a good rest after Christmas so I don't mind that at all and neither does Rudolph.

I will be wearing a mask and will wash my hands or use my sanitiser when I arrive in your house. Please leave my biscuits and milk in a bag for me as I am only allowed to have takeaways and not to stay in your house and eat there.

Mrs Clause, the reindeers and myself are all fit and well but we are in lockdown just now so we sometimes wish we could get out more.

Anyhow, the reason I am writing is to let you know that due to some of the restrictions the elves have had to work from home and have only been able to come into the workshop now and then. We are working as hard as we can despite everything but unfortunately, some toys may not be ready on time for delivery on Christmas Eve. If you do not get everything that you asked for it is not because you are on the naughty list, in fact you have all been great boys and girls in this tough time.

Some of you might get all or most of the things you asked for on Christmas morning. I hope you understand and we will probably send anything missing by post to your Mum and Dad later if we can.

Please be kind to anyone who is missing something and help to make him or her feel better by sharing. I will do my best but some things may not arrive until well after Christmas so please be patient.

Take care, wash your hands and stay in your pods in school. I will be at your house on Christmas Eve but you will not see me, as you will be asleep. I have to go back to work now, lots and lots to do! Love to you all and Happy Holidays,

Santa Clause, North Pole."

Lewis was amazed, he had not thought of Santa and the elves having to work from home like his Mum and Dad or that he might be in lockdown as well. He did not mind if Santa was a little late with some things. He understood and Fionn probably would not notice too much if something he asked for was missing. Lewis smiled up at this Mum and Dad.

"Well what do you think of that, Lewis? Nice of him to take the time to write and I imagine it took a lot of time to talk to every country and get permission to fly in and land. Sure we were not allowed to go away on holidays to Spain this year, remember?"

"Yes," Lewis said excited now. "Do you think Matthew's Mum saw Santa's message?"

"I don't know Lewis but we can ask him tomorrow, can't we?" "Now Dad will bring the two of you up to bed and read you just one story, ok? First brush your teeth well so that the sugar from your cake does not eat them away." Lewis kissed his Mum and stood up. His Dad followed him up the stairs with a sleepy Fionn in his hands.

Lewis felt okay now as his Dad tucked him into bed in the top bunk and Fionn in the bottom bunk. He put on the night light with the stars and planets shining on the ceiling. Lewis fell asleep halfway through the story, content now that all was going to be okay and that Santa was coming. He had lain there planning what he was going to put on his list and did not mind at all that he would have to write it out long hand and post it.

Tomorrow he would see Matthew in the backyard and would have some treats for Halloween. Matthew's costume was that of an astronaut, which Lewis thought was a bit lame but he did not care. It would be fun and maybe it was not so bad not going from house to house as usual.

Lesley Smith

Gratitude

A cool, quiet twilight,

A stately fox, stopped, then passed.

No whisper of breeze, not even a sound,

just a faint perfume of a night scented plant.

The calmness around me reflected my mind,

a deep felt contentment was all I could find.

The silence a companion, the touch on my skin,

my heart beating slowly a rhythm within.

Each day is a gift each moment a jewel,

The pace reduced, so strange and new.

So take time to ponder before we move on,

the world is recovering, wonder not gone.

Drink in the moments, don't miss the change,

realise that we can hear bird song again.

Lesley Smith

Author Biographies

Mairead de Bhal

Mairead de Bhal has been a member of Gorey Writers for the last three years. Published with them in their recent Anthology, she previously published in her twenties when she worked as a freelance journalist, in Dublin and London.

Returning to writing at this point in her life has been a joy for her. She enjoys the magic of it.

She has rediscovered the thrill of sea swimming and the great outdoors, with family and friends, during the Covid Pandemic restrictions.

Mark Rice

Mark Rice has been writing short stories for many years and in 2017 published his first novel "Murder In Maspalomas". He followed it up with "Murder On Board" published by Junction Publishing in 2019 and has another novel targeted for release in early 2021. All his books are currently available on Amazon and Kindle. He is the eldest of four brothers and lives with his wife in County Wexford, Ireland. He has taken up the ukulele in recent years and has threatened to compose songs in the coming year. His blog is weirdorwhat.wordpress.com.

Lesley Smith

Lesley Smith has been writing poems and short stories since she was a child. She trained as a nurse and worked in health for more than thirty years. Lesley lived in both the UK and Switzerland for a short while and is a Francophile with ties to a port town close to the border between France and Spain (Port Vendres). Lesley was born and reared one of five children in an Irish protestant family. The works included are written in this year, whilst living in the Dublin suburbs. Further poetry by Lesley are viewable at www.lesleysmithpoetry.com

Printed in Poland
by Amazon Fulfillment
Poland Sp. z o.o., Wrocław

64226319R00107